BENNY
AND
PENNY

IN
JUST PRETEND

A TOON BOOK BY
GEOFFREY HAYES

TOON BOOKS IS AN IMPRINT OF CANDLEWICK PRESS

BOOKLIST TOP 10 GRAPHIC NOVELS FOR YOUTH

MARYLAND BLUE CRAB YOUNG READERS HONOR BOOK

BANK STREET COLLEGE OF EDUCATION
Best Children's Books of the Year

KIRKUS BEST OF '09 CONTINUING SERIES

IOWA GOLDFINCH AWARD

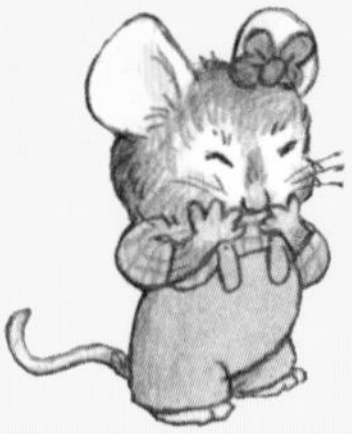

For Françoise

Editorial Director: FRANÇOISE MOULY

Book Design: FRANÇOISE MOULY & JONATHAN BENNETT

GEOFFREY HAYES' artwork was drawn in colored pencil.

 Printed in Dongguan, Guangdong, China by Toppan Leefung. Library of Congress Control Number: 2007941867. ISBN: 978-0-9799238-0-7 (hardcover)

ISBN: 978-1-935179-26-9 (paperback)

13 14 15 16 17 18 TPN 10 9 8 7 6 5 4 3 2 1

WWW.TOON-BOOKS.COM

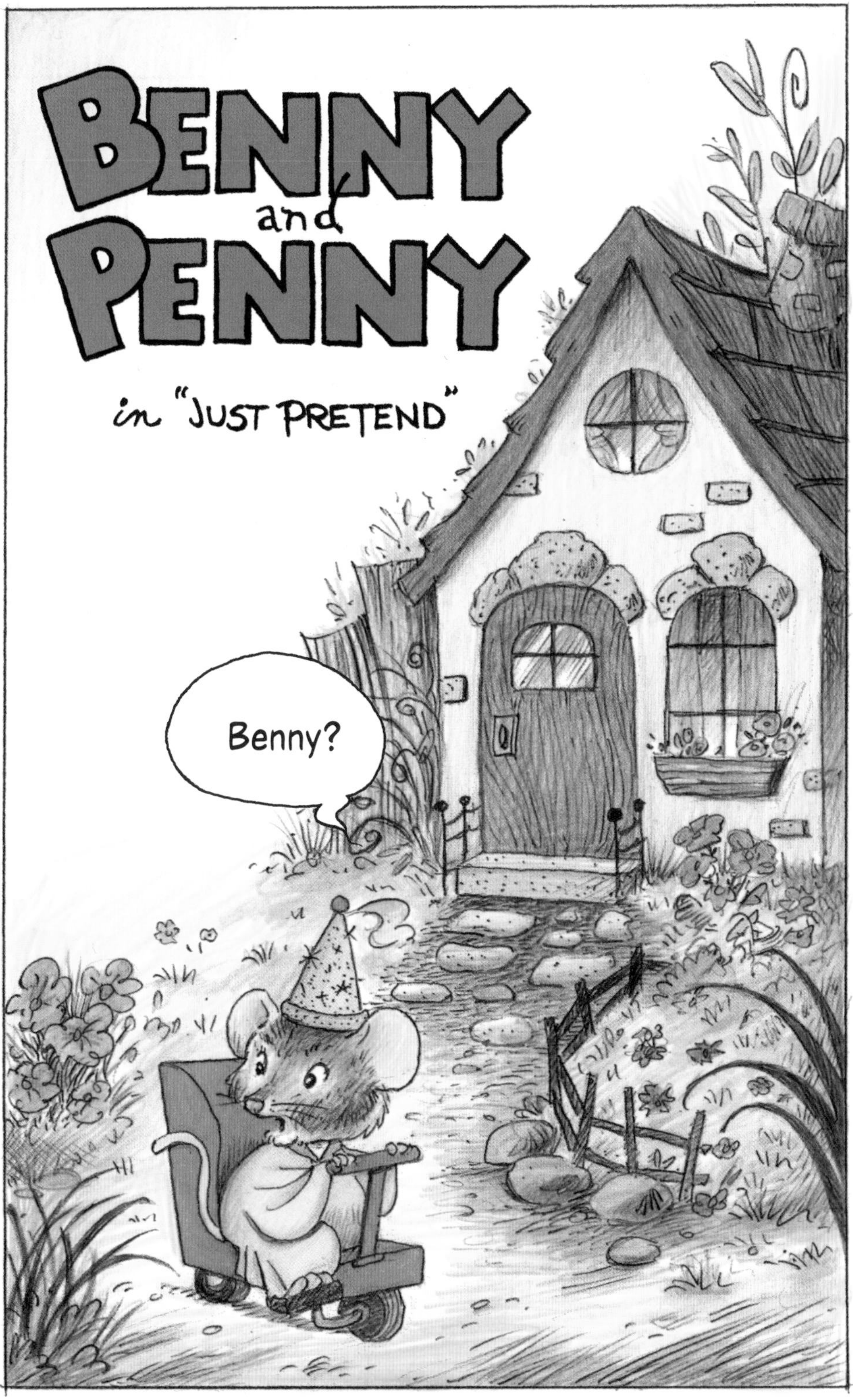
BENNY and PENNY
in "JUST PRETEND"
Benny?

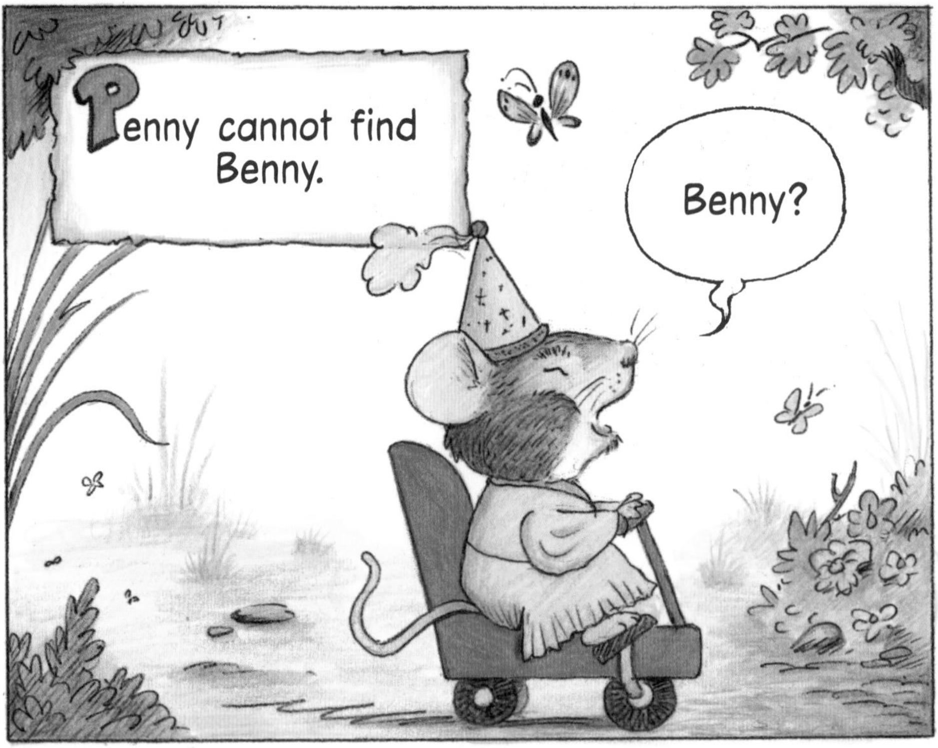
Penny cannot find Benny.
Benny?

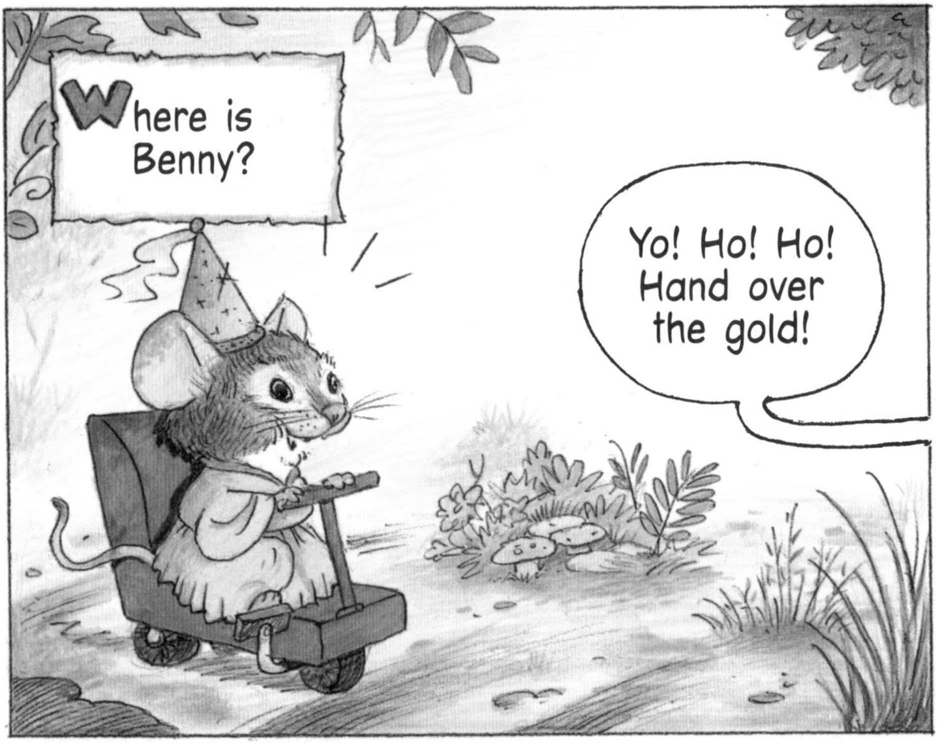
Where is Benny?
Yo! Ho! Ho! Hand over the gold!

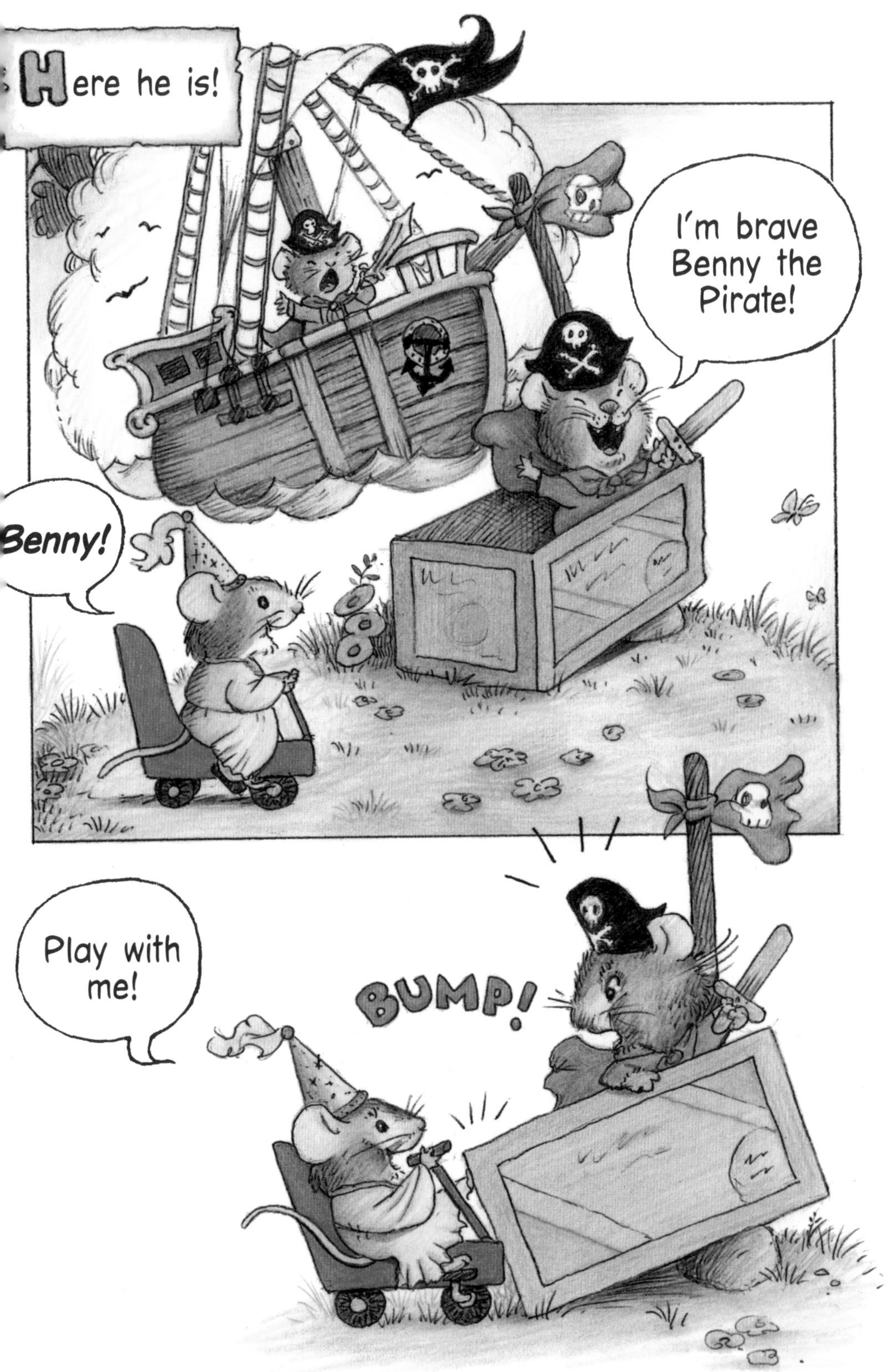
Here he is!
I'm brave Benny the Pirate!
Benny!
Play with me!
BUMP!

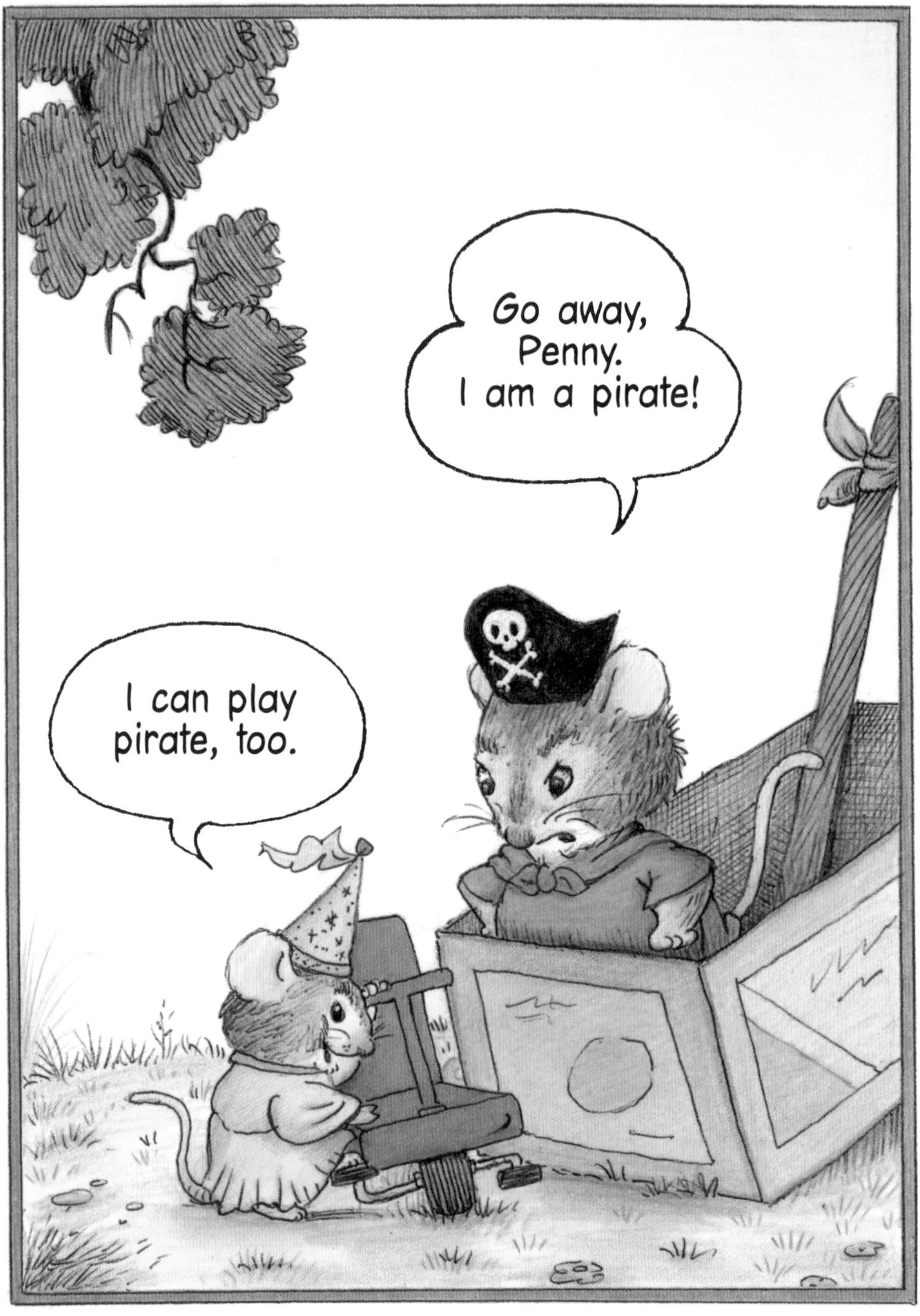
Go away, Penny. I am a pirate!
I can play pirate, too.

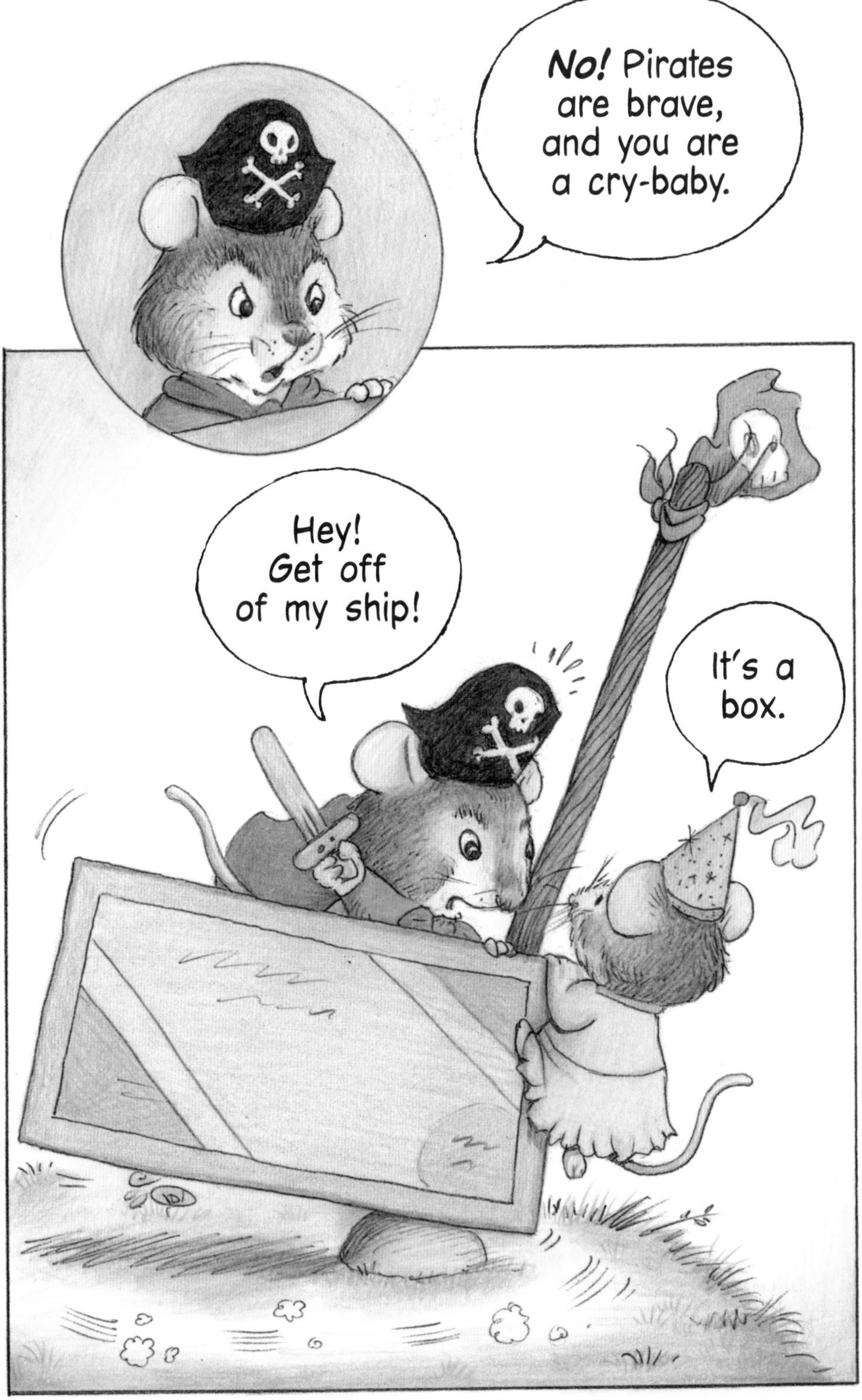
No! Pirates are brave, and you are a cry-baby.
Hey! Get off of my ship!
It's a box.

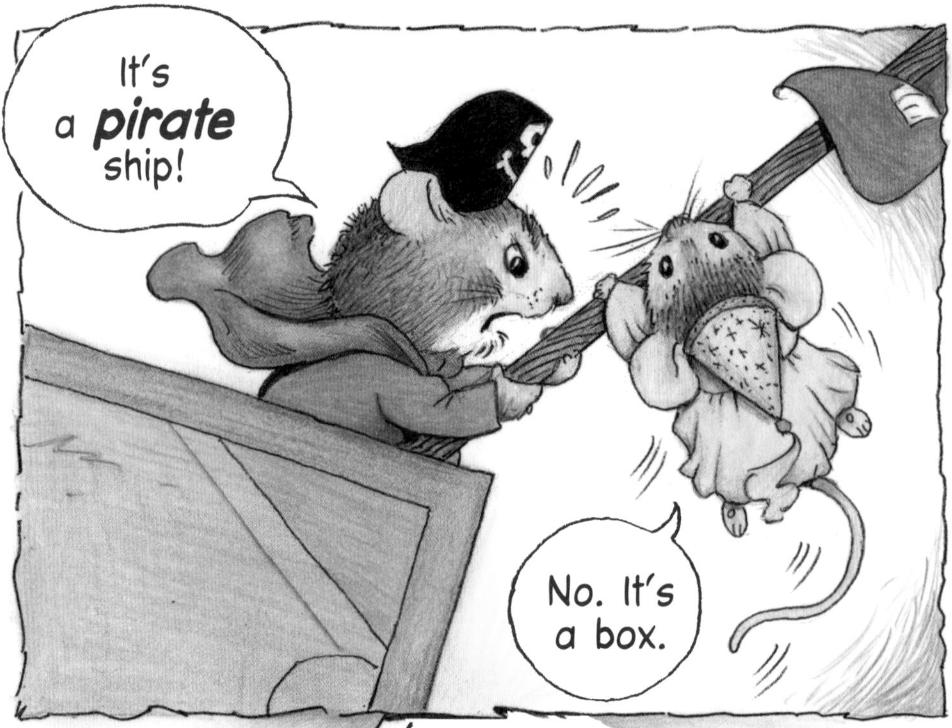
It's a pirate ship!
No. It's a box.

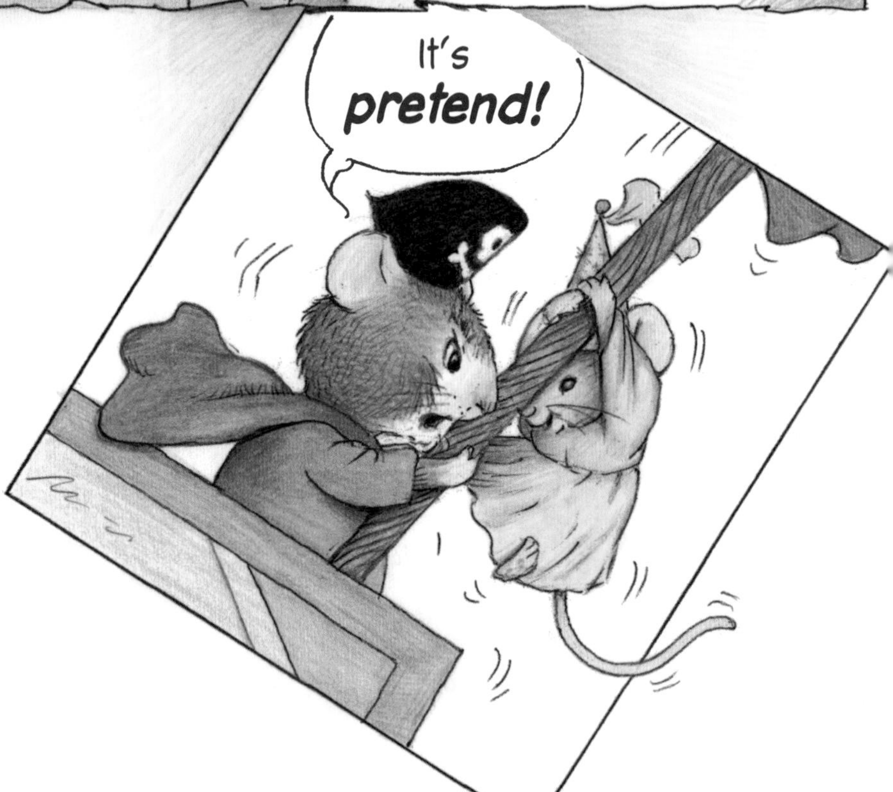
It's pretend!

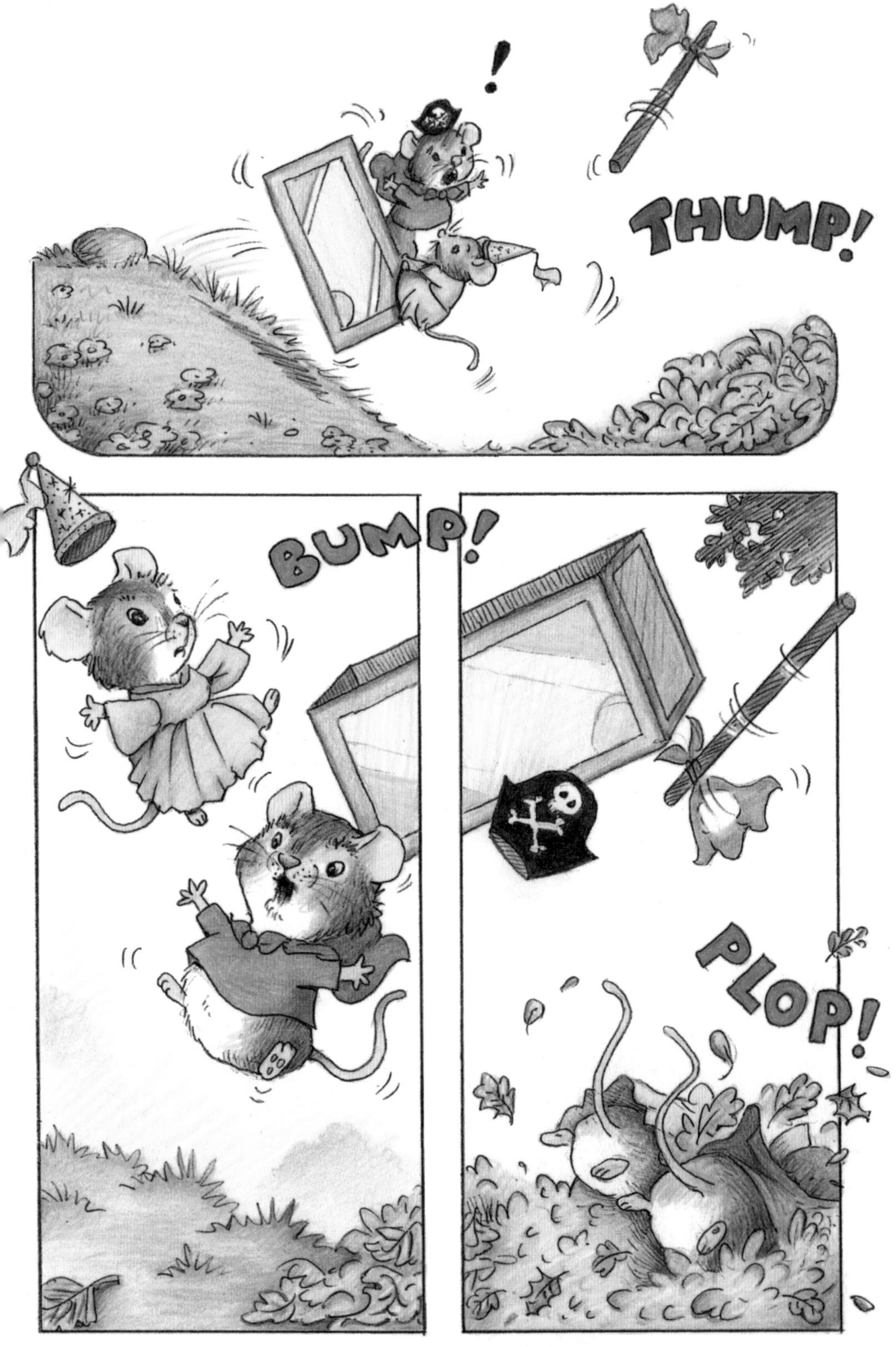
!
THUMP!
BUMP!
PLOP!

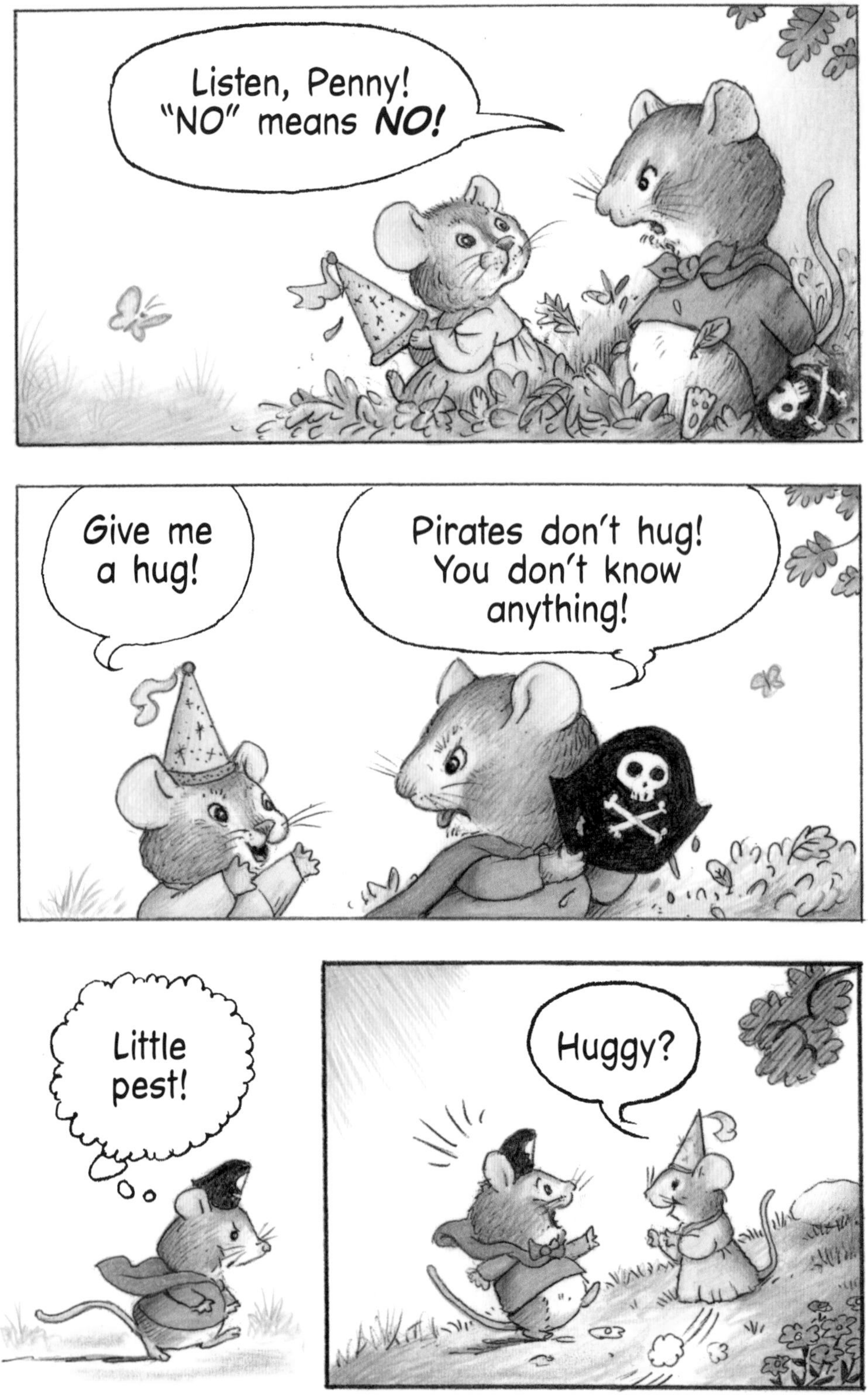
Listen, Penny! "NO" means NO!
Give me a hug!
Pirates don't hug! You don't know anything!
Little pest!
Huggy?

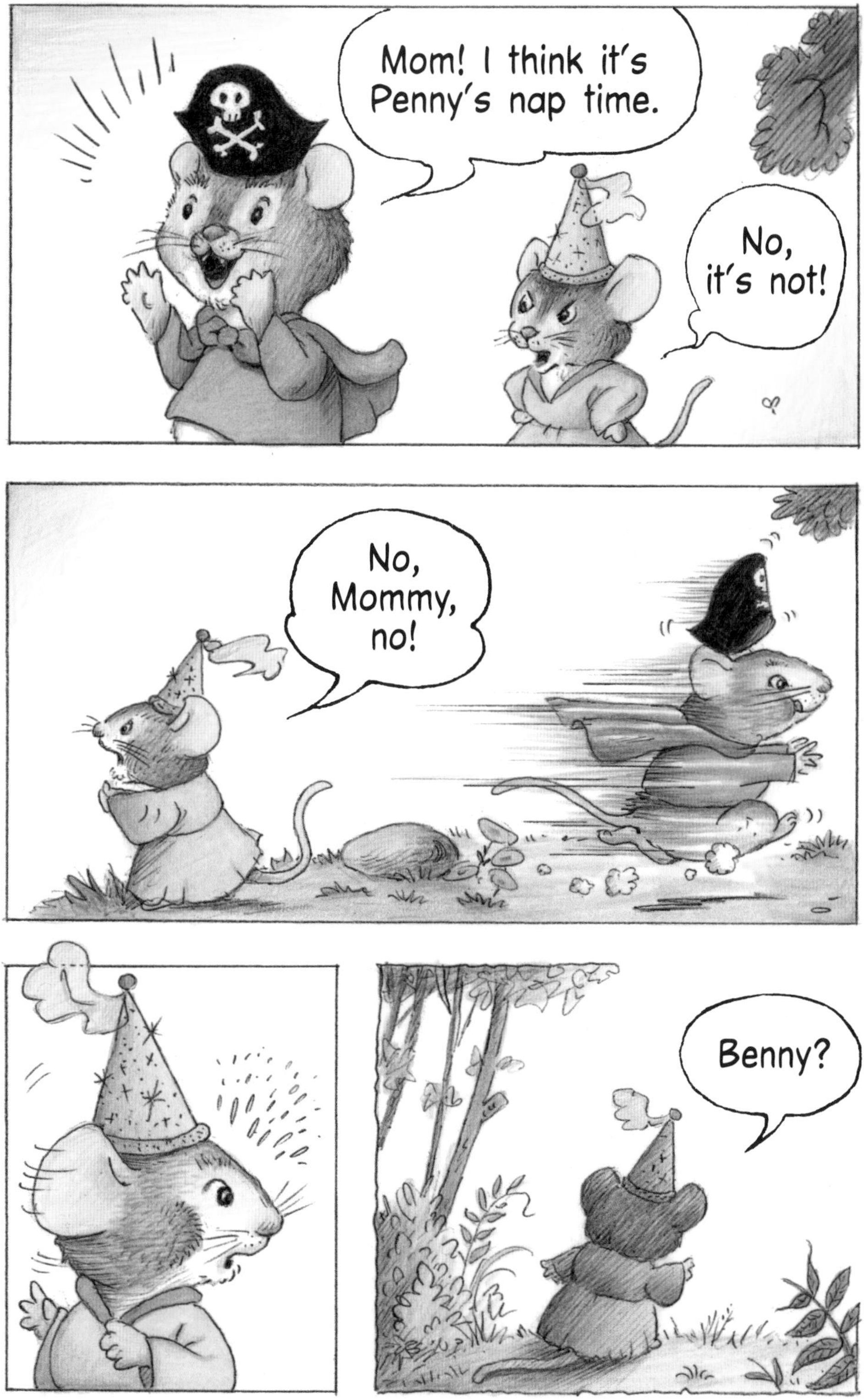
Mom! I think it's Penny's nap time.
No, it's not!
No, Mommy, no!
Benny?

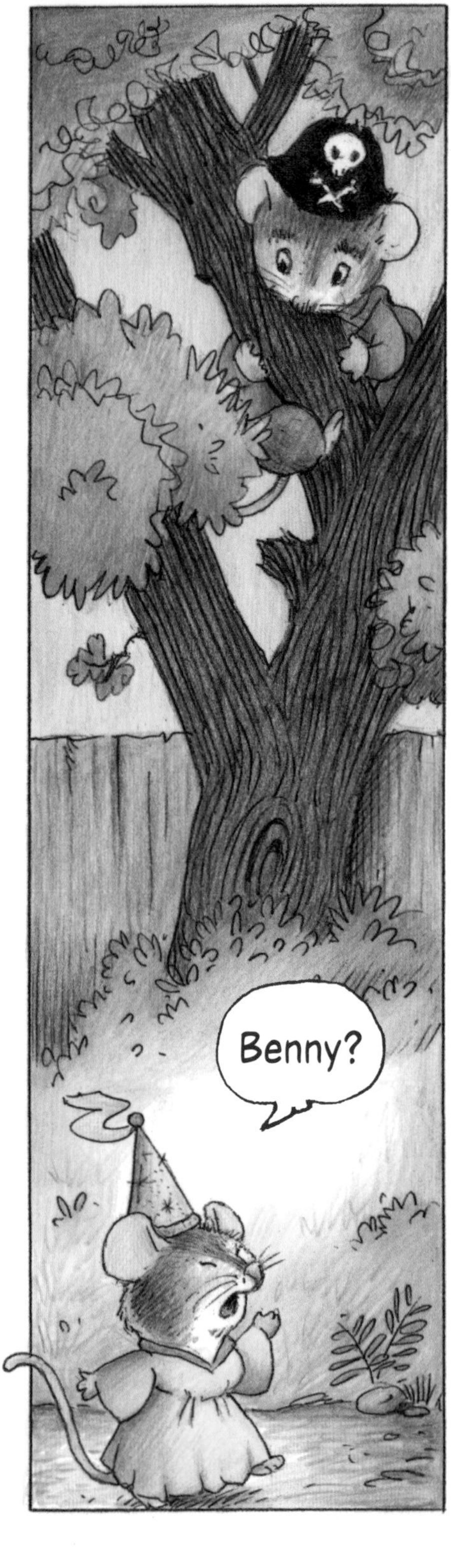
Benny?

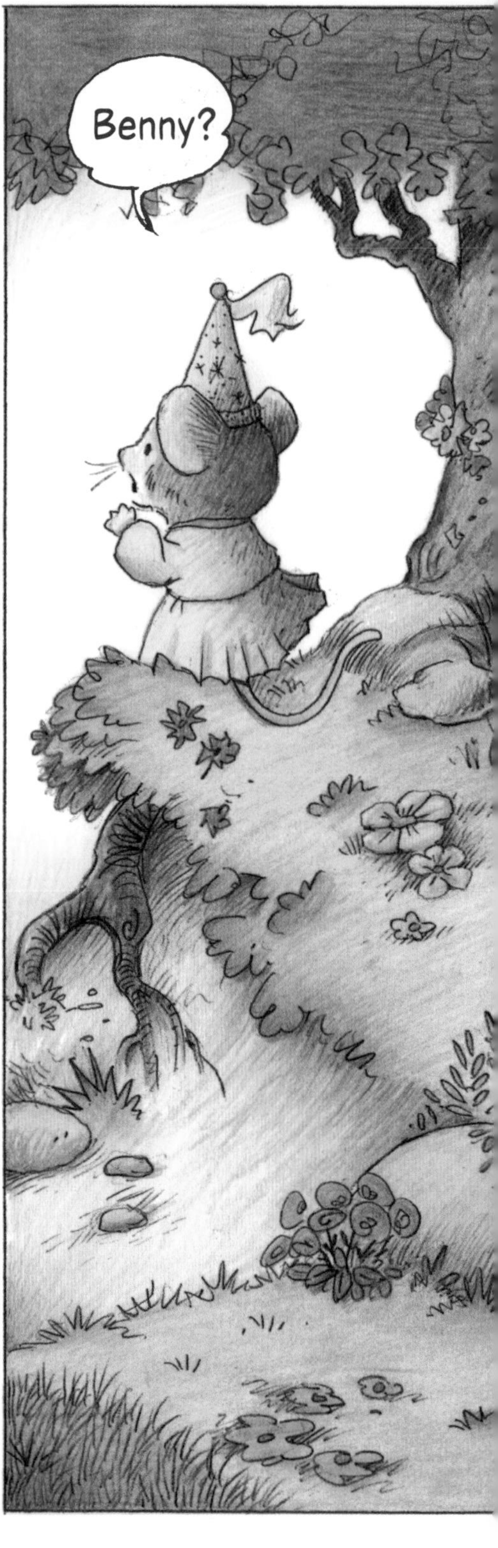
Benny?

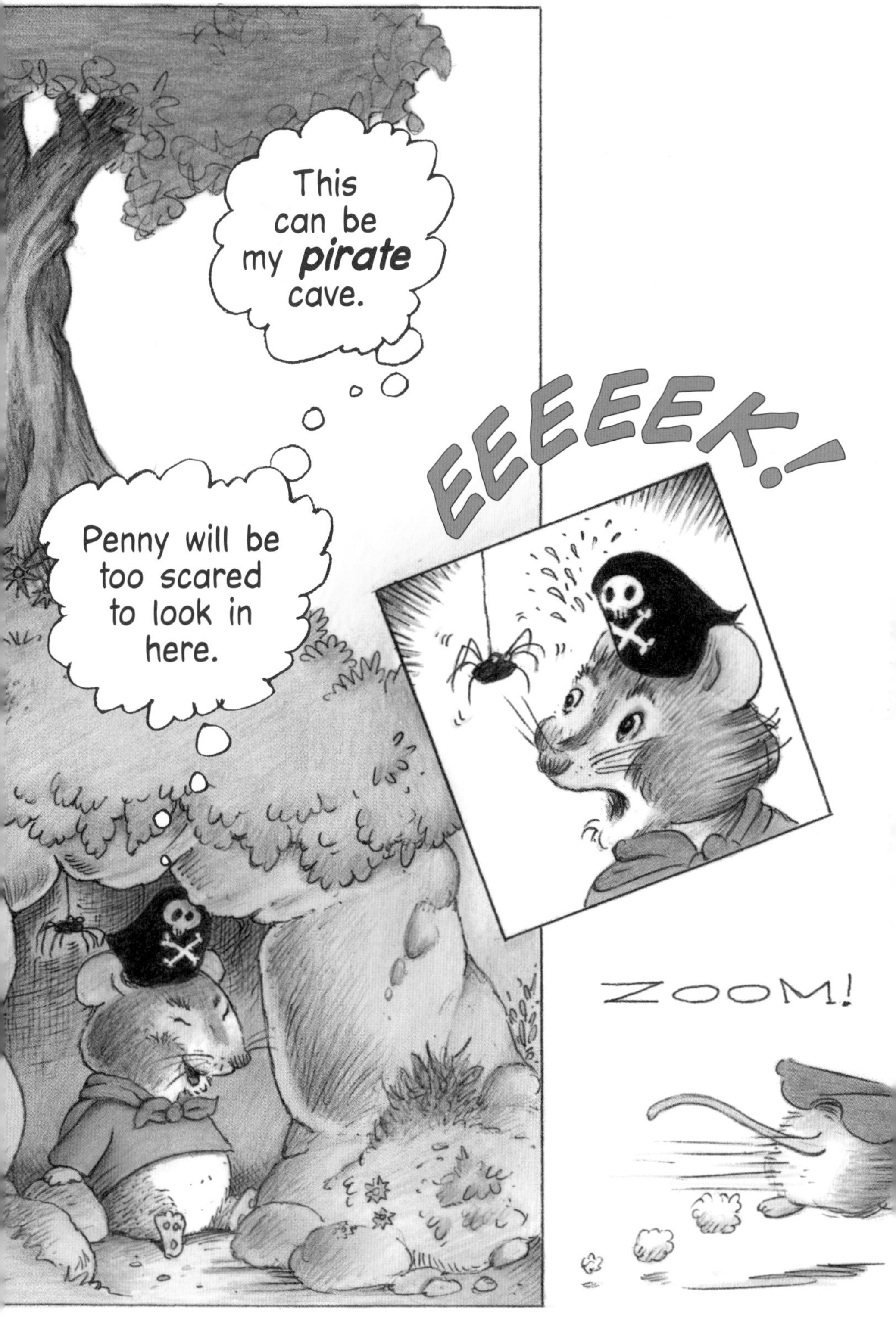
This can be my *pirate* cave.
Penny will be too scared to look in here.
EEEEEK!
ZOOM!

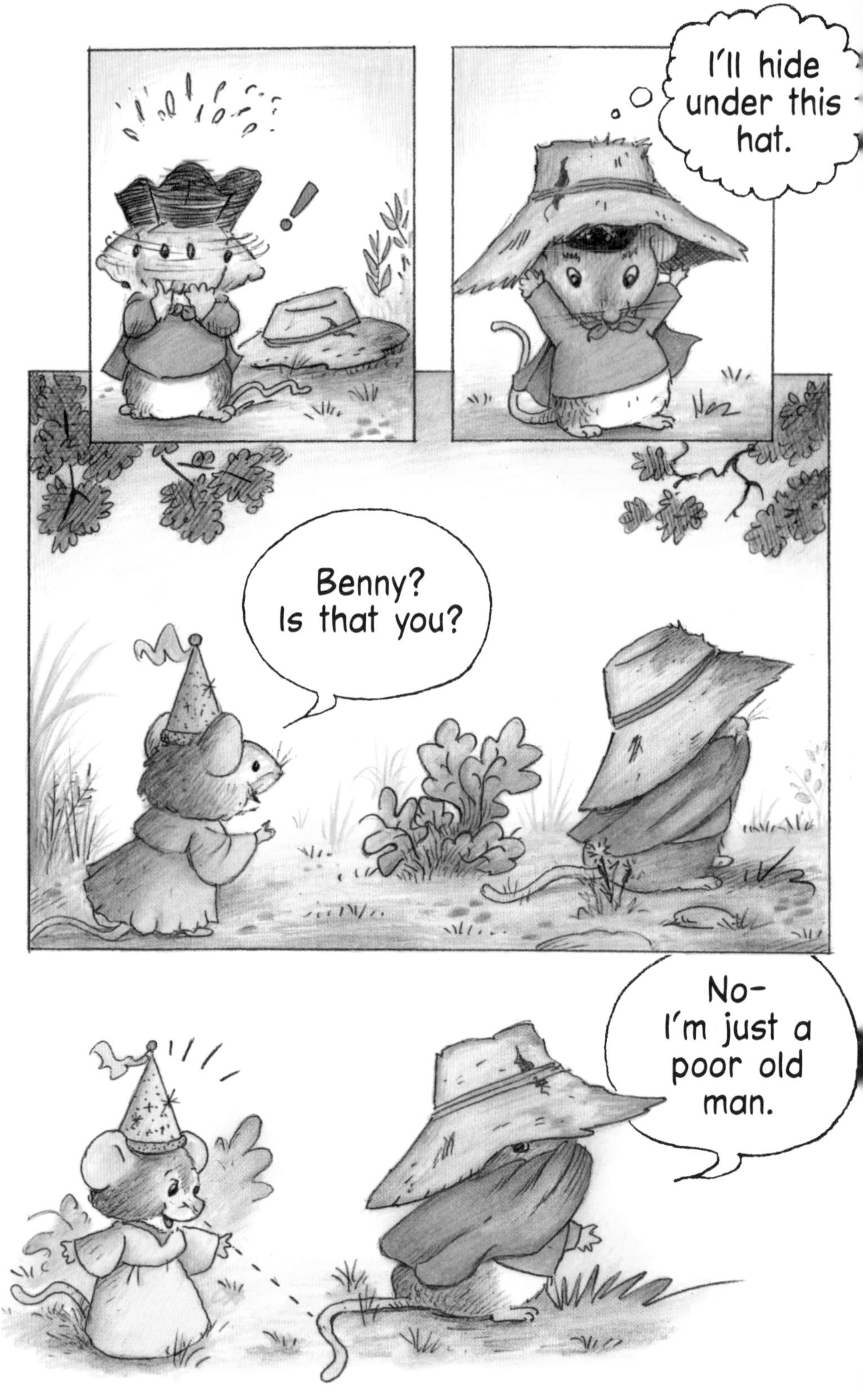
I'll hide under this hat.
Benny? Is that you?
No– I'm just a poor old man.

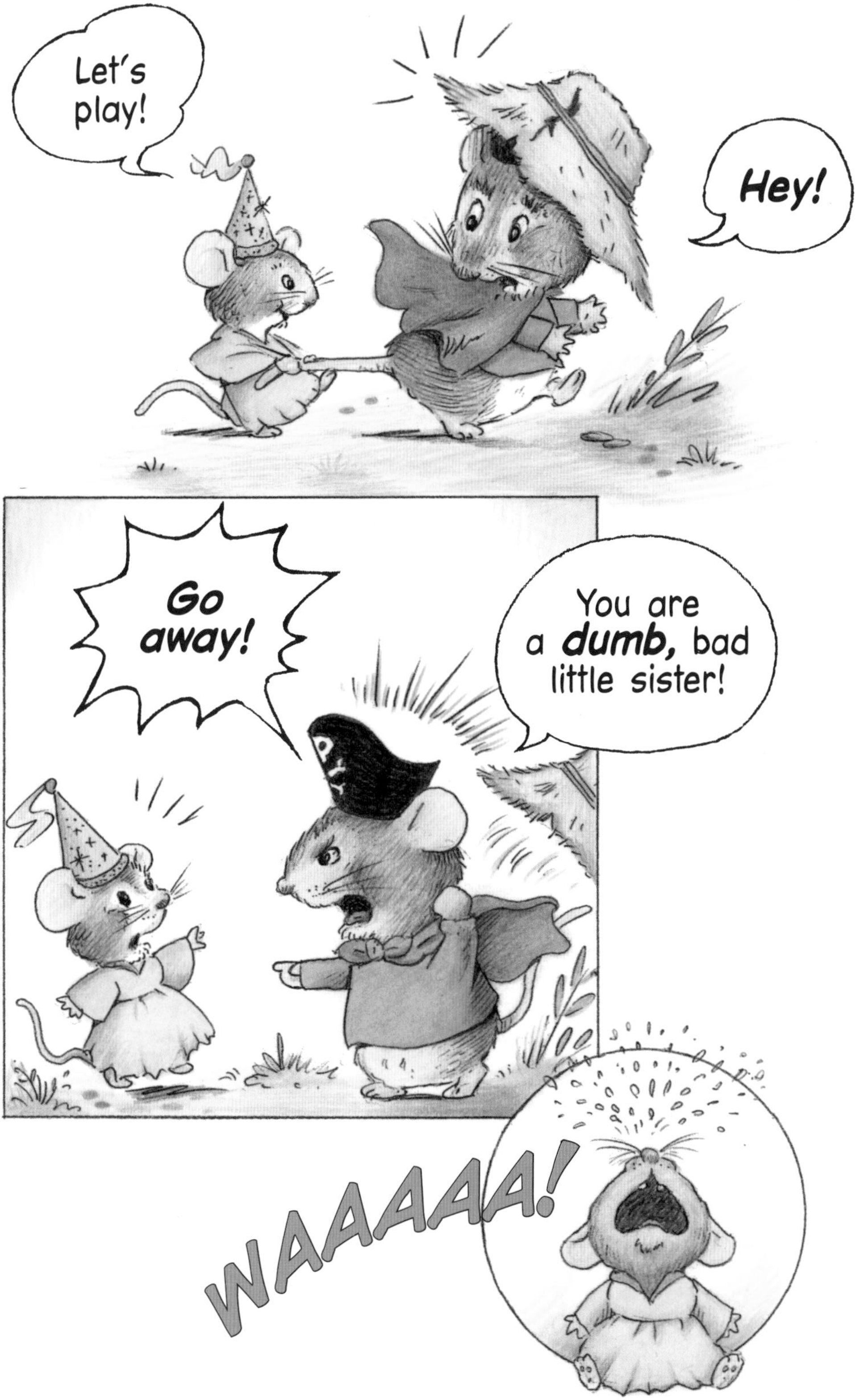
Let's play!
Hey!
Go away!
You are a **dumb,** bad little sister!
WAAAAA!

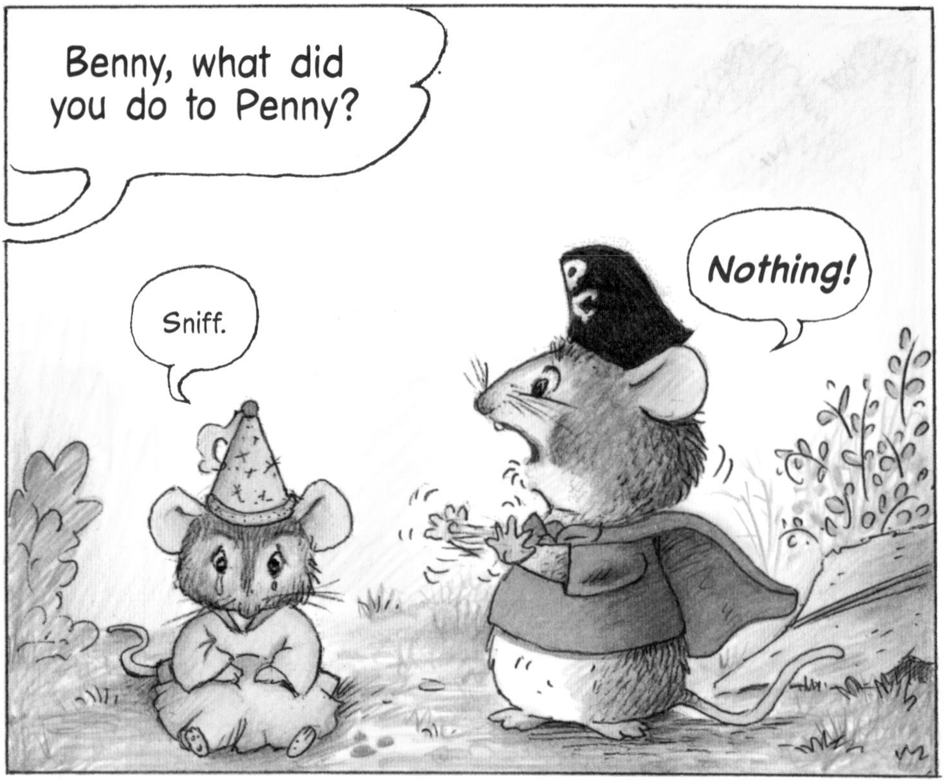
Benny, what did you do to Penny?
Sniff.
Nothing!

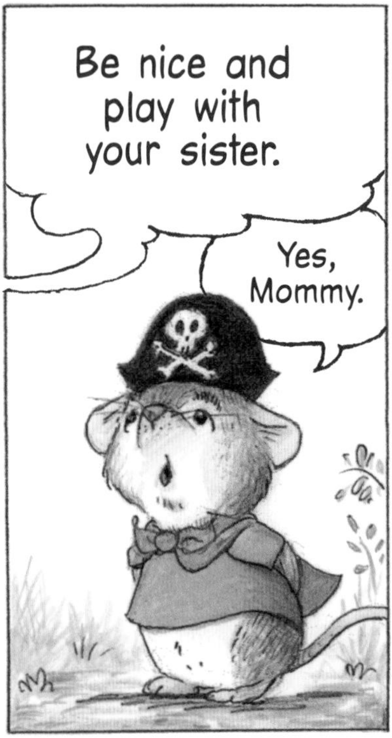
Be nice and play with your sister.
Yes, Mommy.

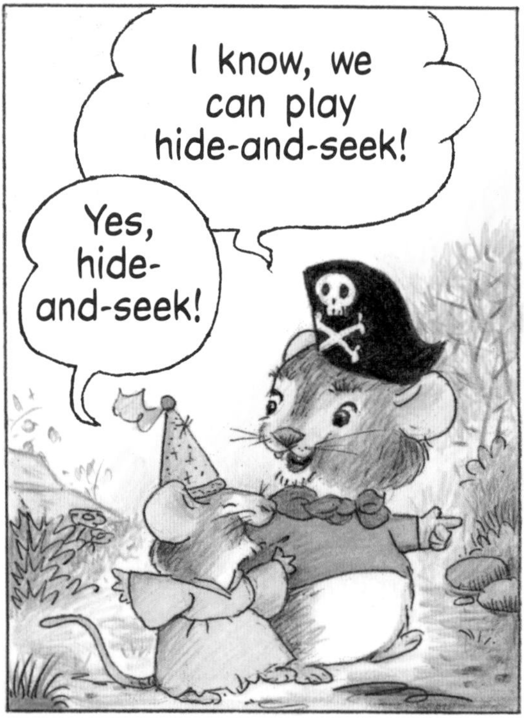
I know, we can play hide-and-seek!
Yes, hide-and-seek!

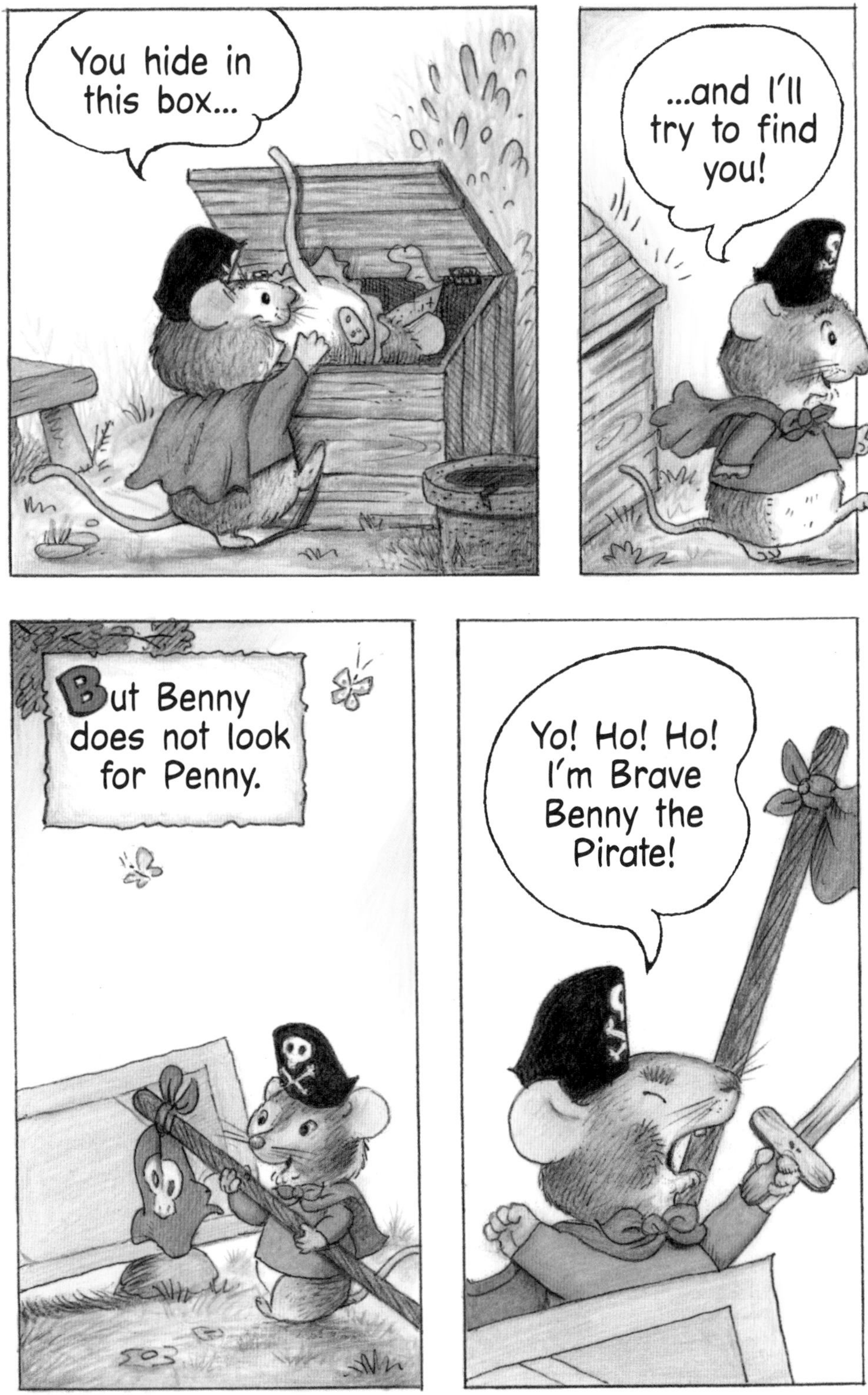
You hide in this box...
...and I'll try to find you!
But Benny does not look for Penny.
Yo! Ho! Ho! I'm Brave Benny the Pirate!

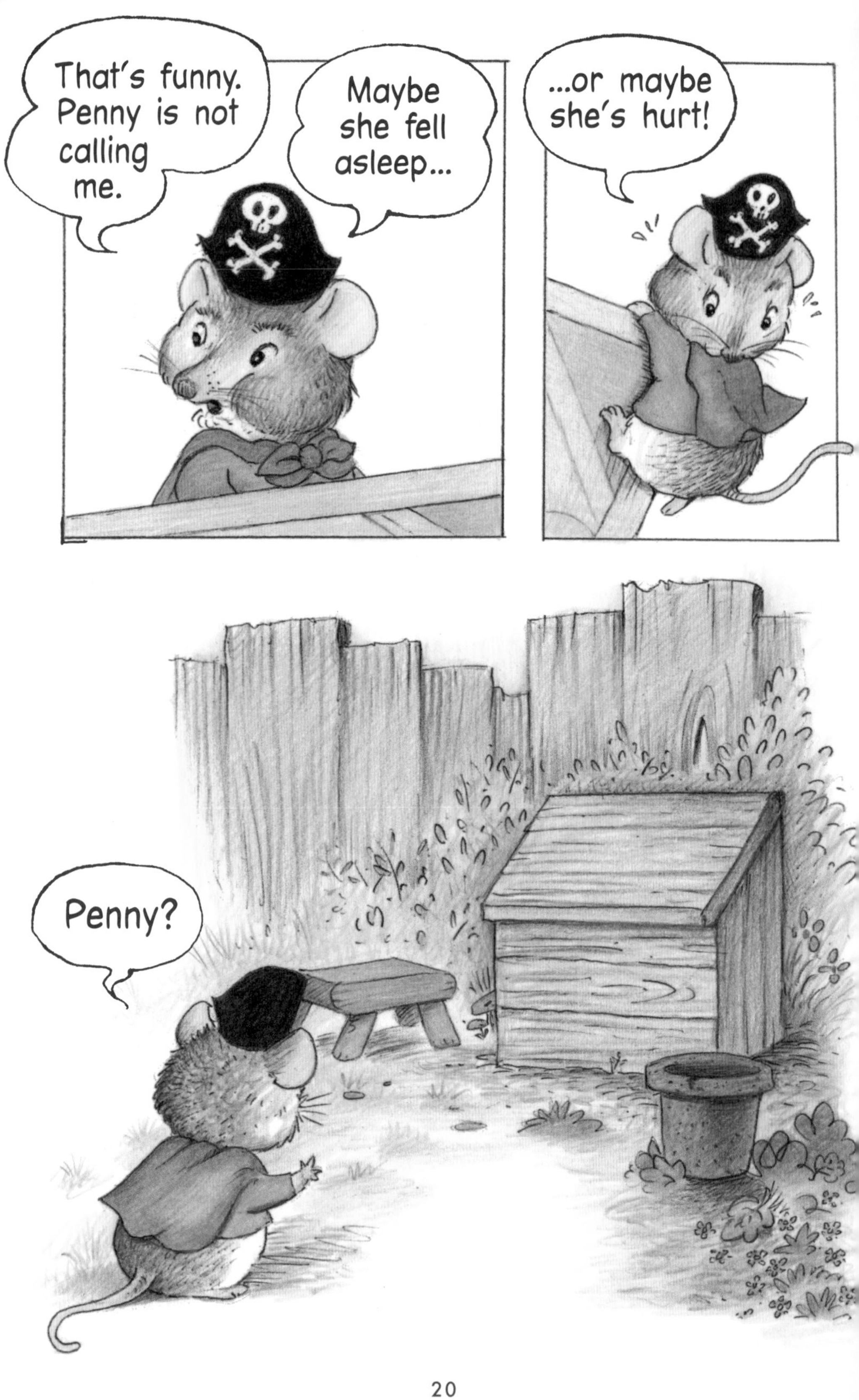
That's funny. Penny is not calling me.
Maybe she fell asleep...
...or maybe she's hurt!
Penny?

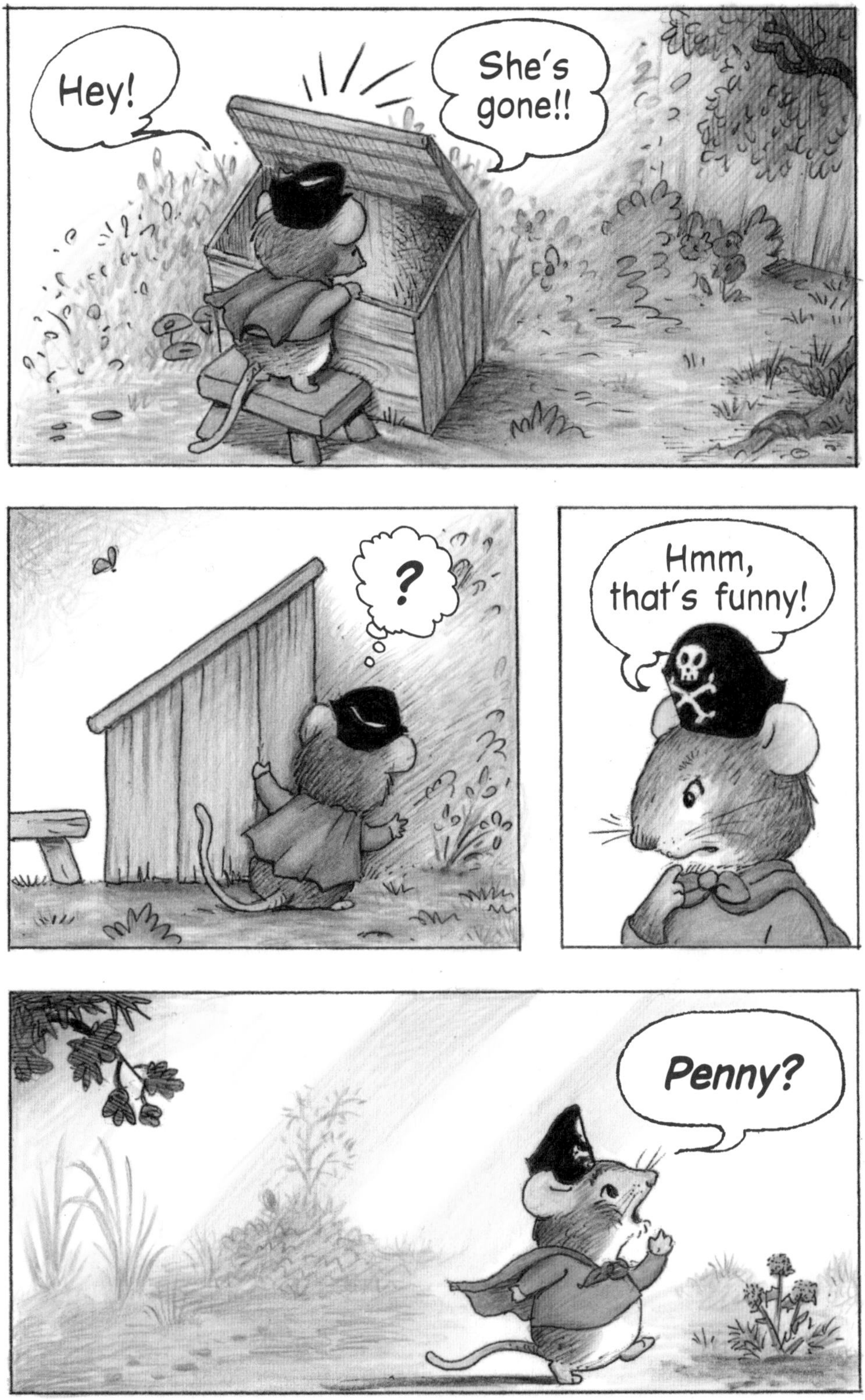
Hey!
She's gone!!
?
Hmm, that's funny!
Penny?

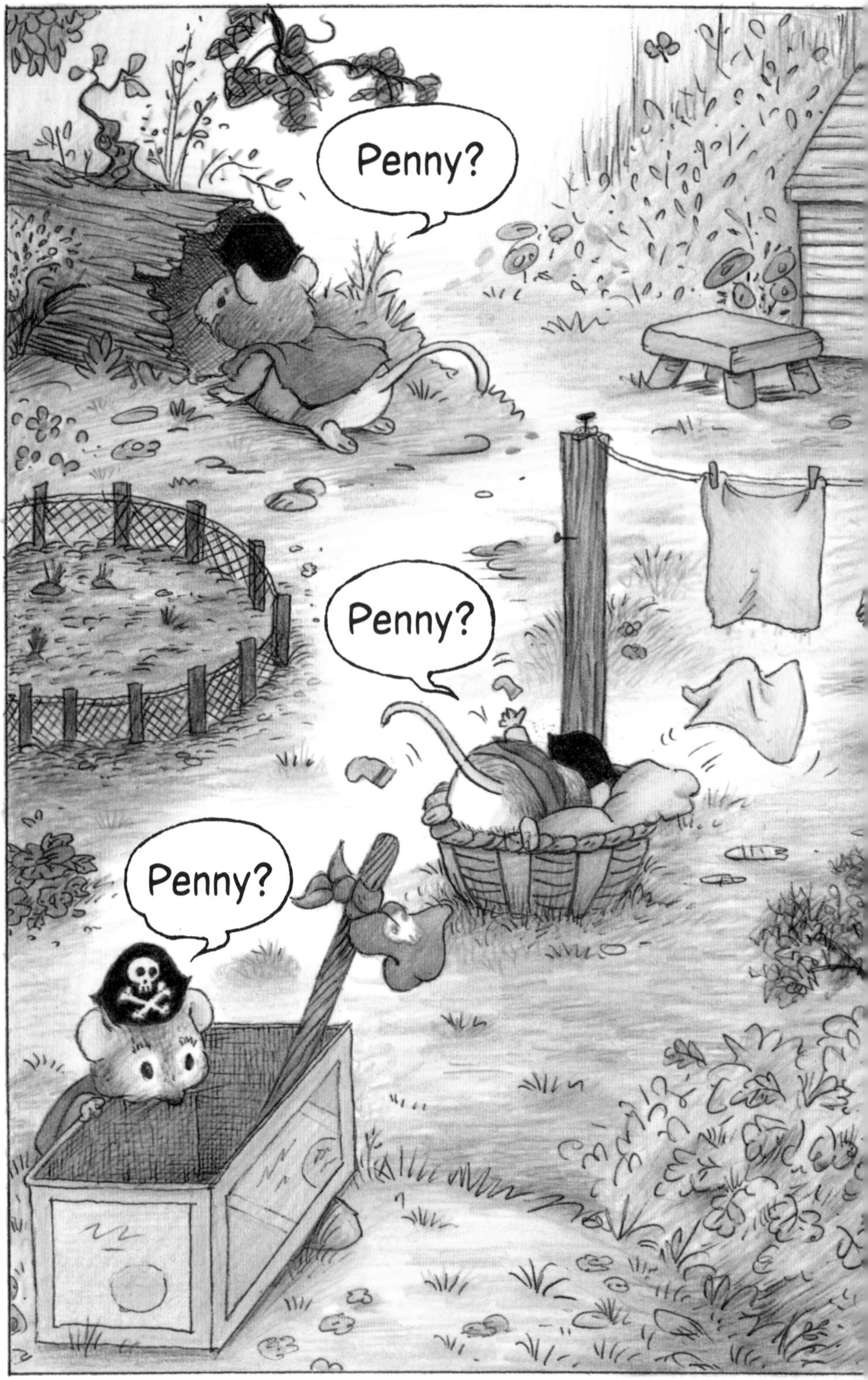
Penny?
Penny?
Penny?

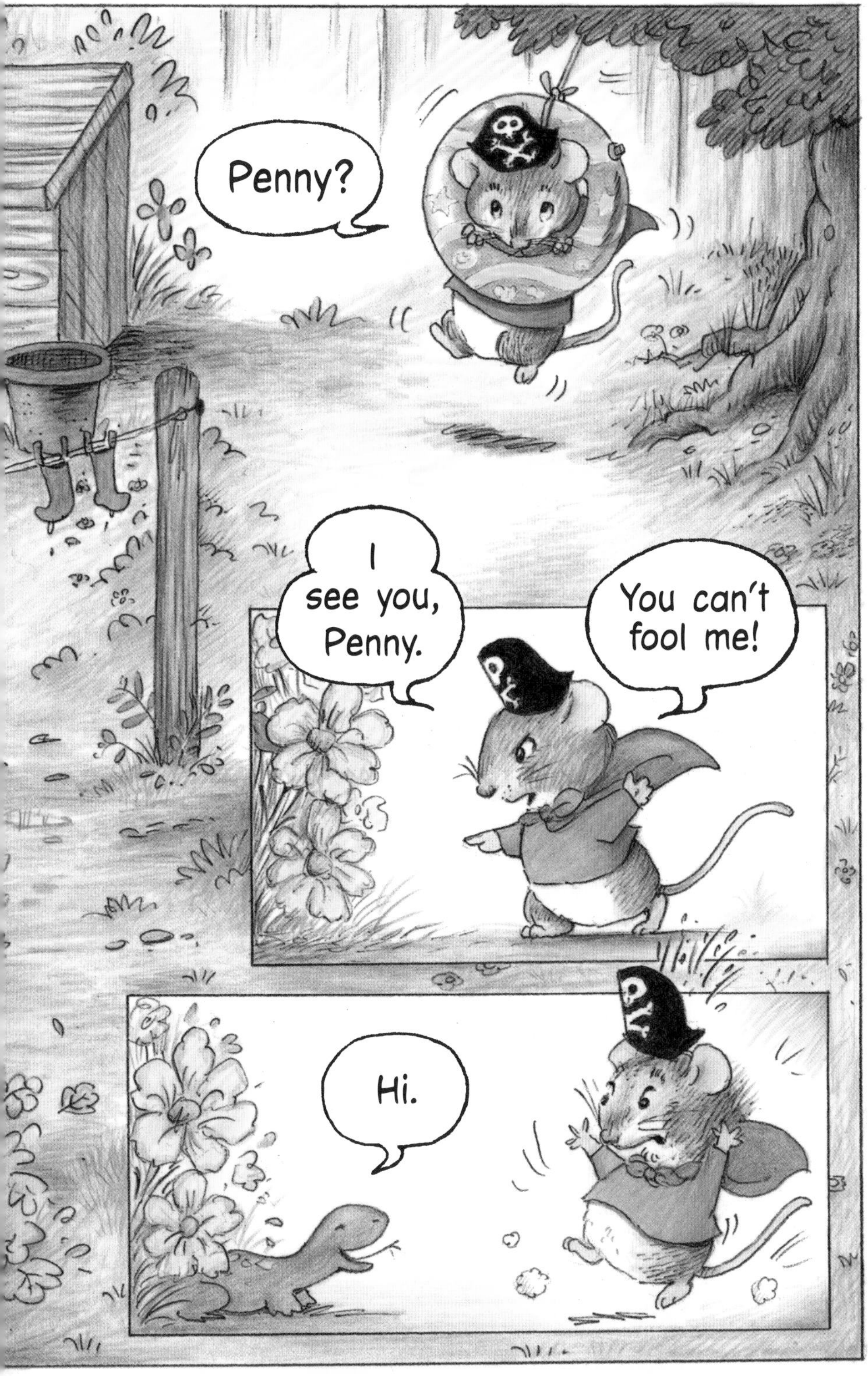
Penny?
I see you, Penny.
You can't fool me!
Hi.

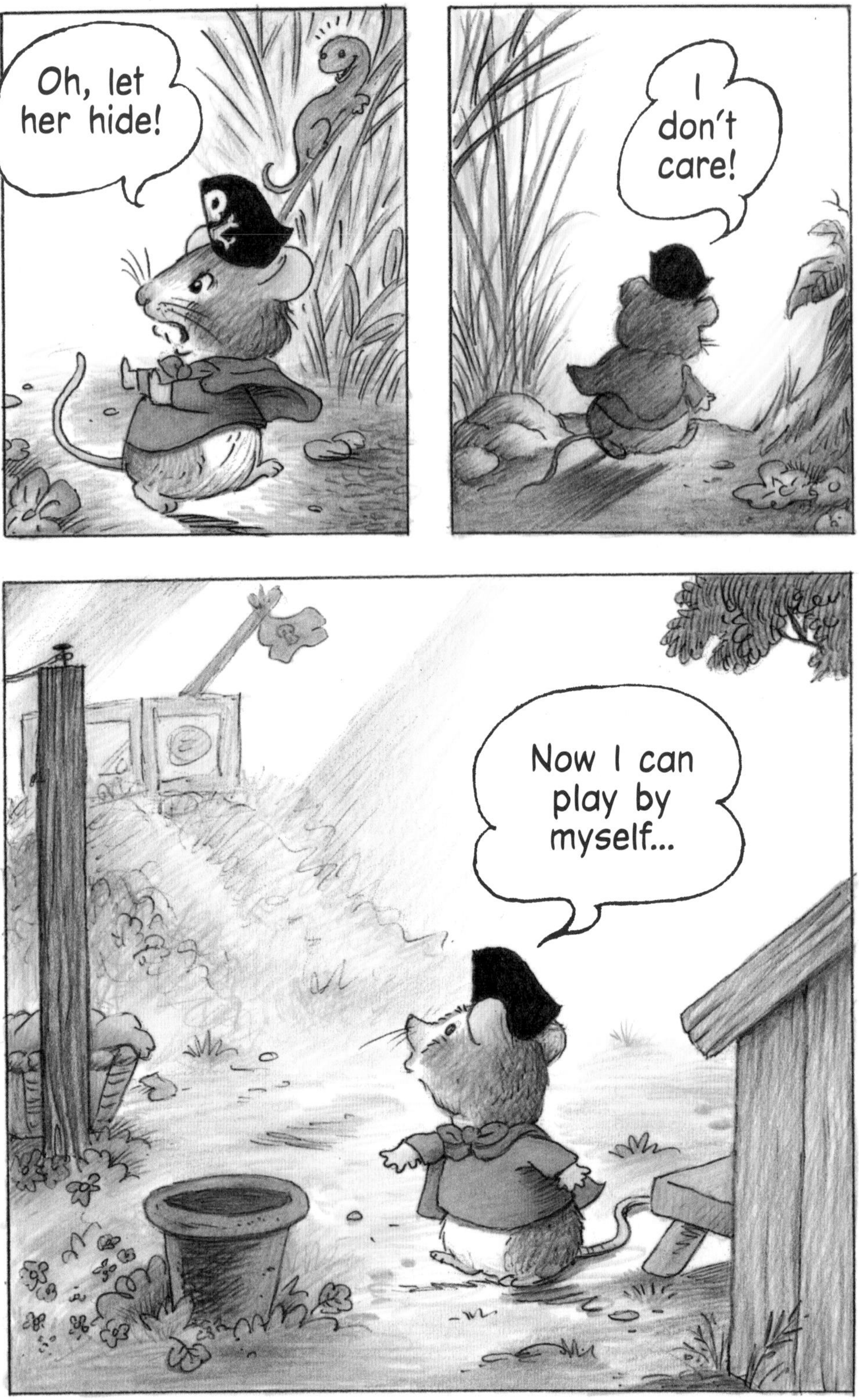
Oh, let her hide!
I don't care!
Now I can play by myself...

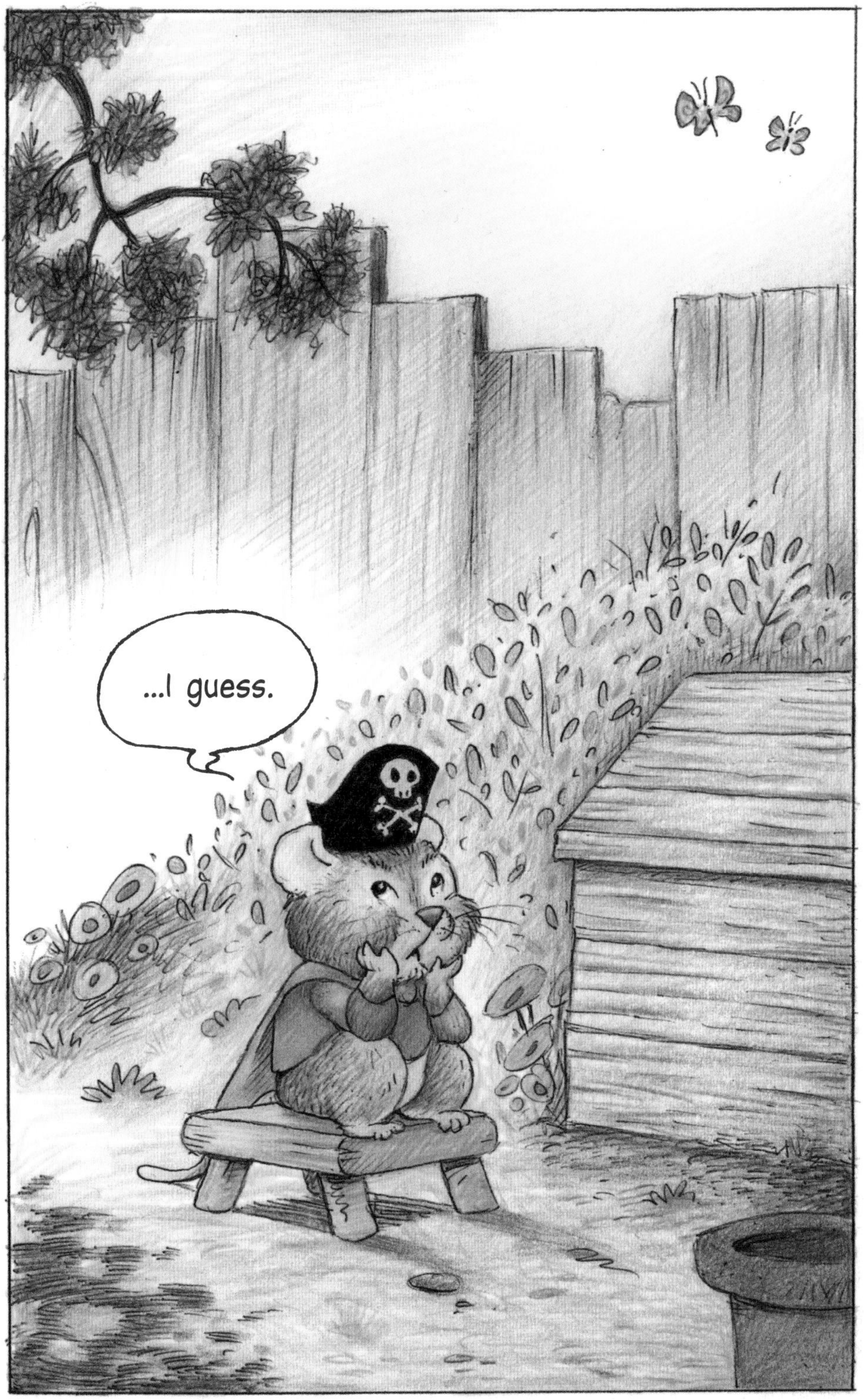
...I guess.

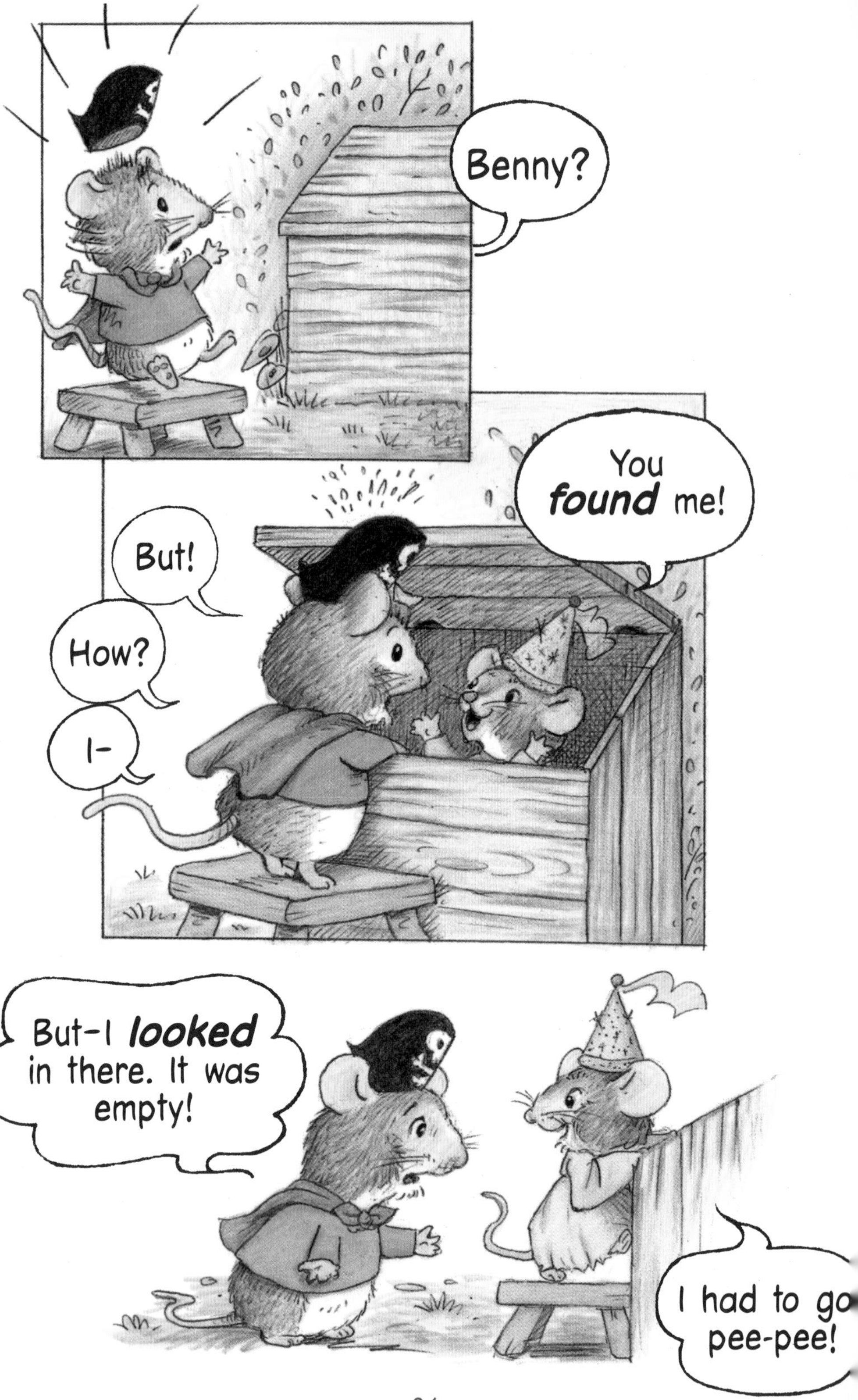
Benny?
You **found** me!
But!
How?
I-
But-I **looked** in there. It was empty!
I had to go pee-pee!

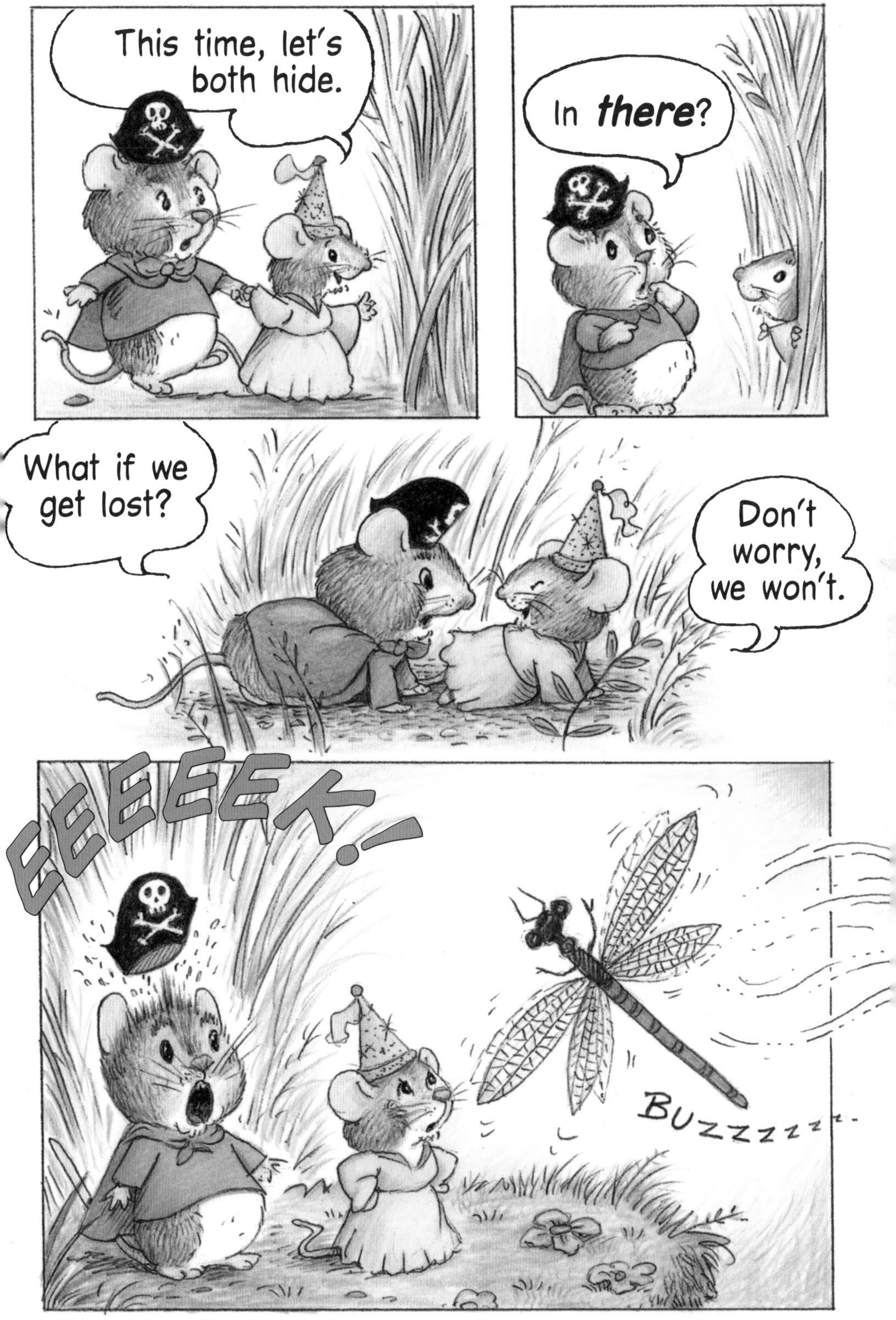
This time, let's both hide.
In *there*?
What if we get lost?
Don't worry, we won't.
EEEEEK!
BUZZZZZZ..

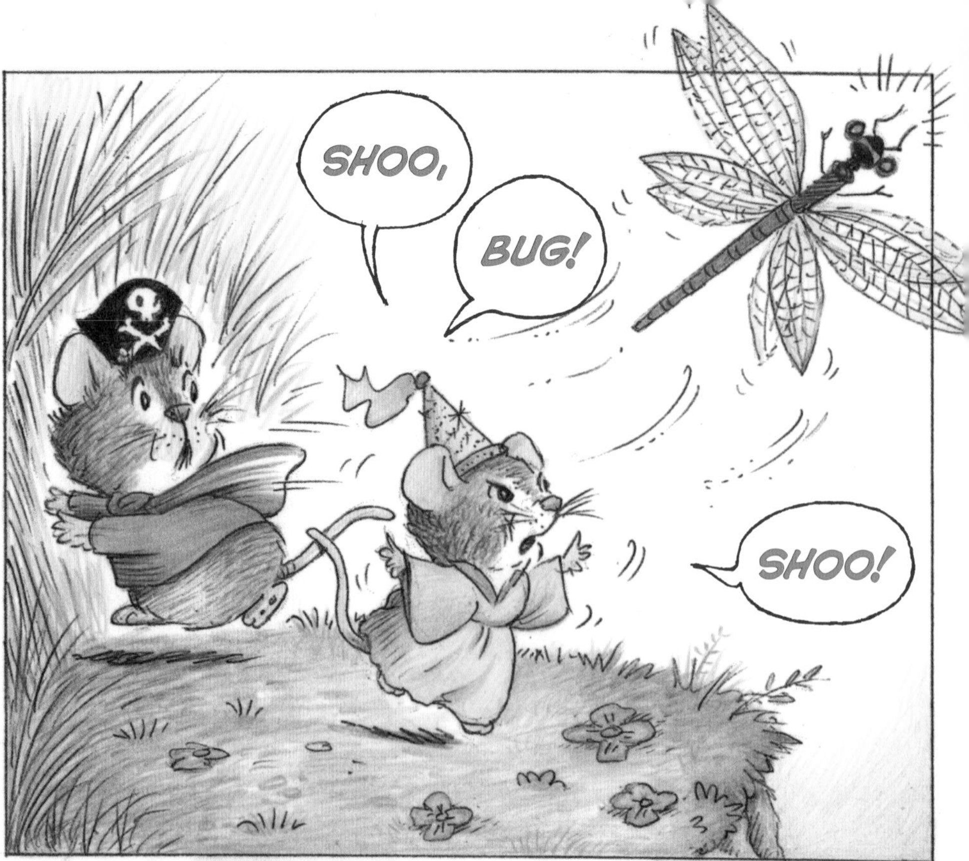
SHOO,
BUG!
SHOO!

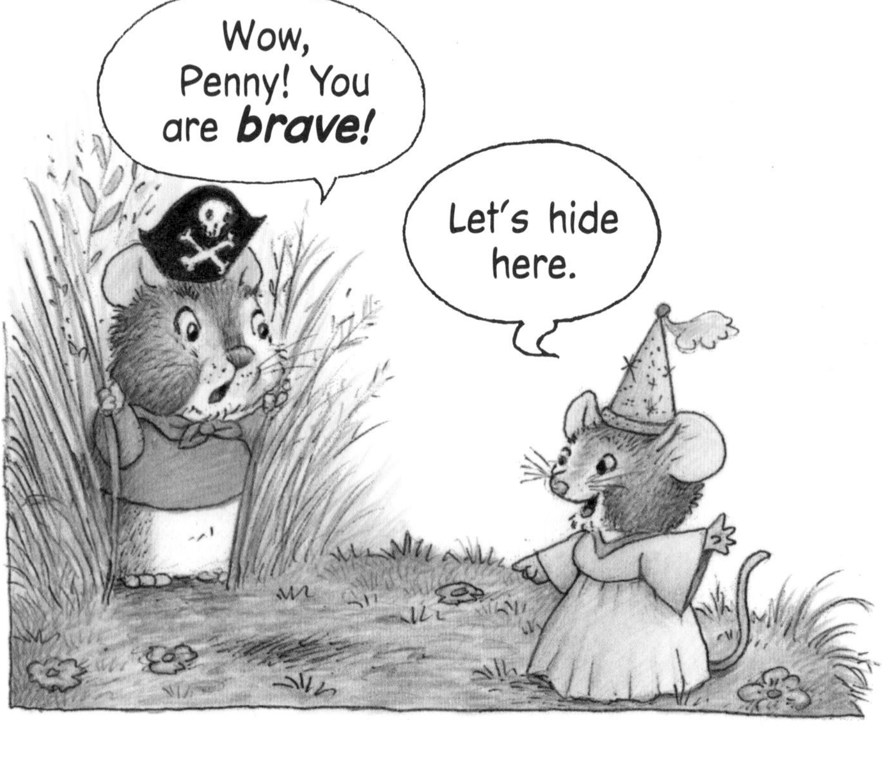
Wow, Penny! You are ***brave!***
Let's hide here.

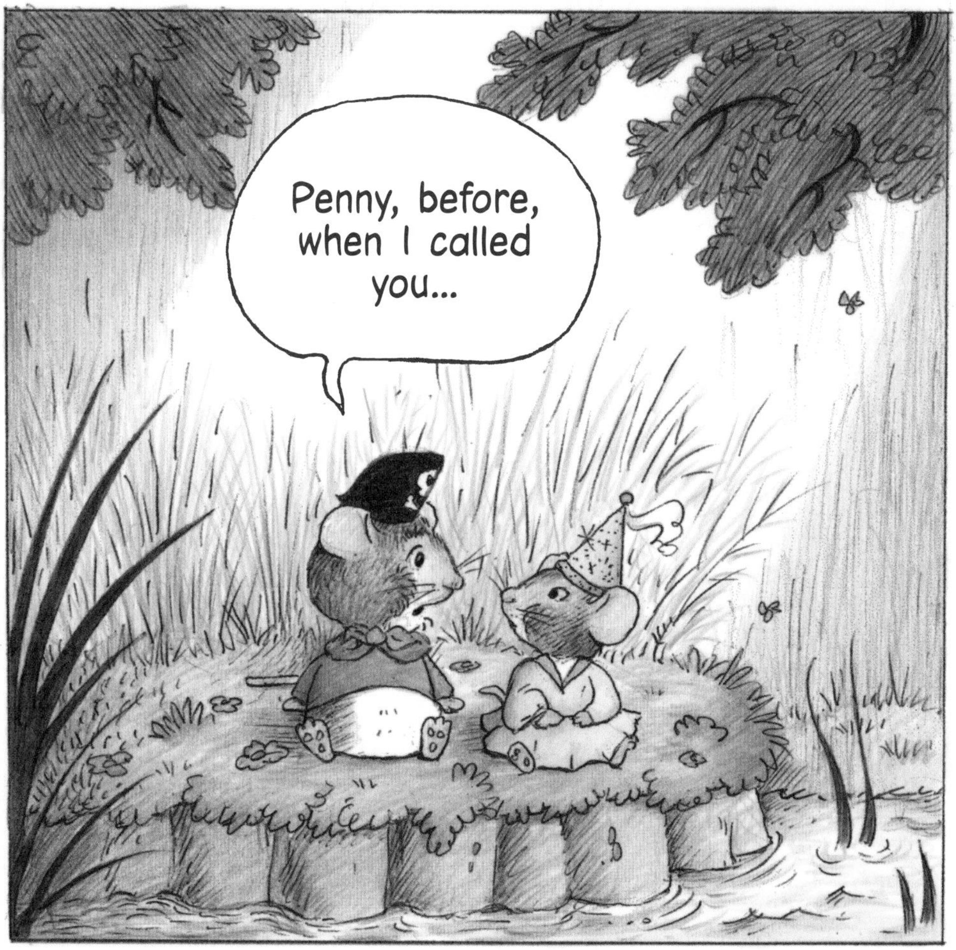
Penny, before, when I called you...

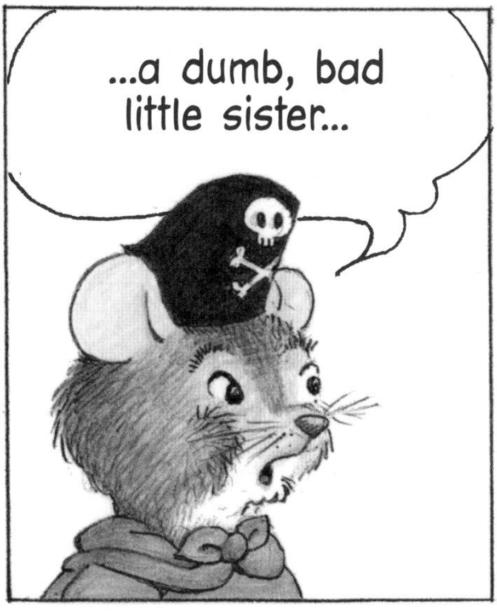
...a dumb, bad little sister...

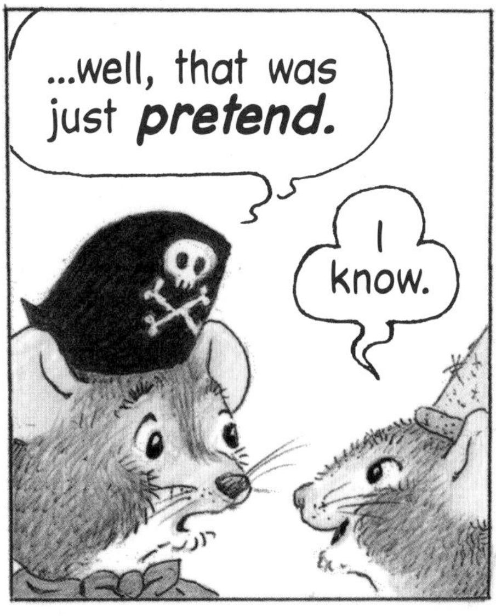
...well, that was just **pretend.**
I know.

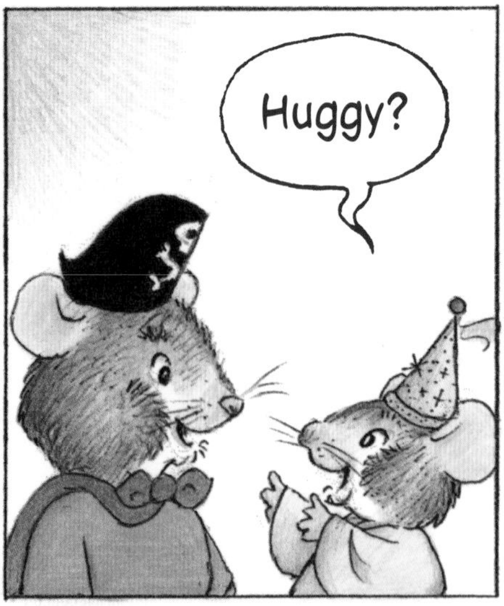
Huggy?

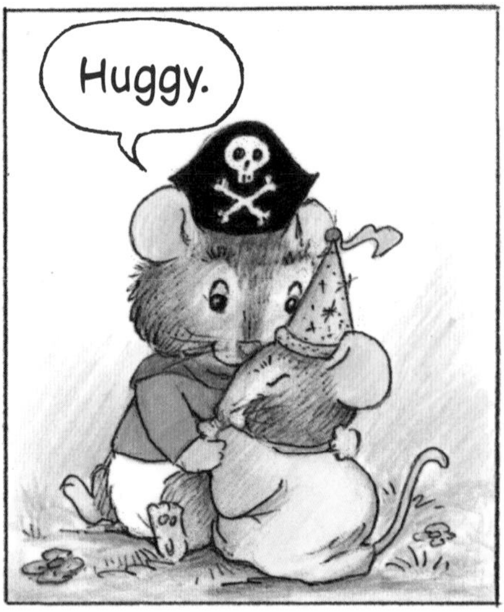
Huggy.

And where are Benny and Penny now?

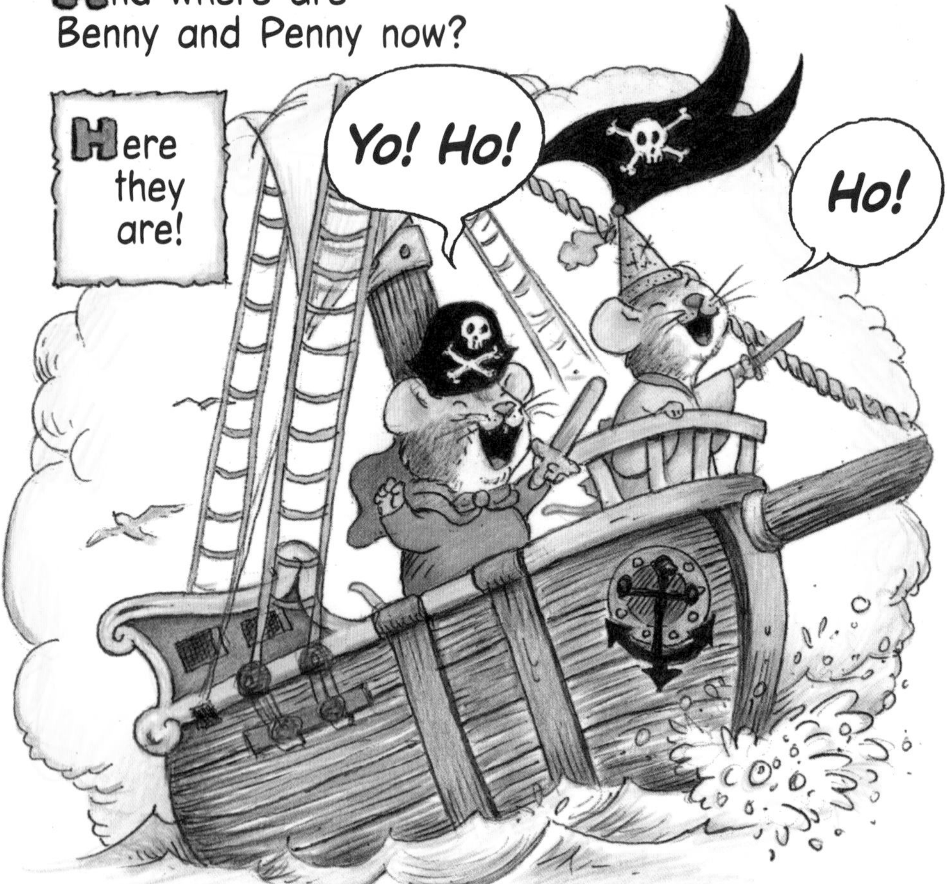
Here they are!
Yo! Ho!
Ho!

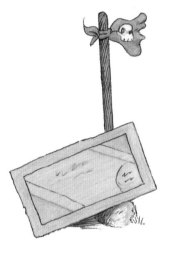

THE END

ABOUT THE AUTHOR

Geoffrey grew up in San Francisco, where he still lives. From an early age, he and his younger brother Rory wrote and illustrated stories for one another.

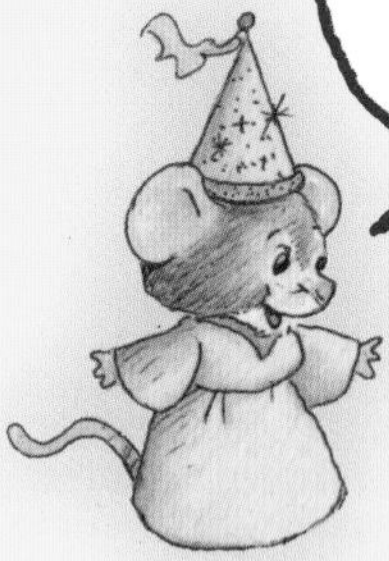

Geoffrey says, "Like *Benny* I often wanted to play alone. But when I gave in to Rory's demands that I play with him, I was always glad that I did." Both Geoffrey and Rory grew up to be artists.

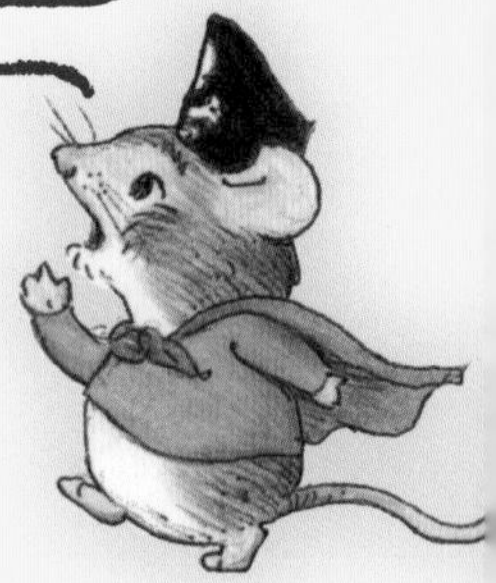

Geoffrey has written and illustrated over forty children's books, among them the classic *Bear By Himself* and *When the Wind Blew* by Margaret Wise Brown. He is the author of the extremely successful series of early readers *Otto and Uncle Tooth*.

HOW TO "TOON INTO READING"

in a few simple steps:

Our goal is to get kids reading—and we know kids LOVE comics. We publish award-winning early readers in comics form for elementary and early middle school, and present them in three levels.

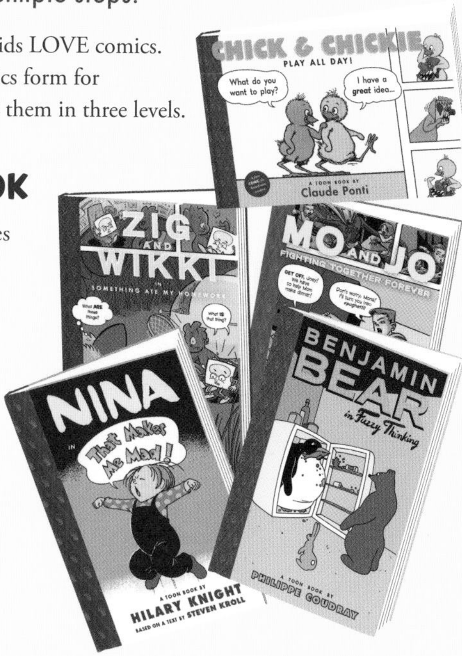

CHICK & CHICKIE
PLAY ALL DAY!
What do you want to play?
I have a great idea...
A TOON BOOK BY
Claude Ponti
ZIG AND WIKKI
IN SOMETHING ATE MY HOMEWORK
MO AND JO
FIGHTING TOGETHER FOREVER
NINA
IN That Makes Me Mad!
A TOON BOOK BY
HILARY KNIGHT
BASED ON A TEXT BY STEVEN KROLL
BENJAMIN BEAR
in Fuzzy Thinking
A TOON BOOK BY
PHILIPPE COUDRAY

① FIND THE RIGHT BOOK

Veteran teacher Cindy Rosado tells what makes a good book for beginning and struggling readers alike: "A vetted vocabulary, plenty of picture clues, repetition, and a clear and compelling story. Also, the book shouldn't be too easy—or the reader won't learn, but neither should it be too hard—or he or she may get discouraged."

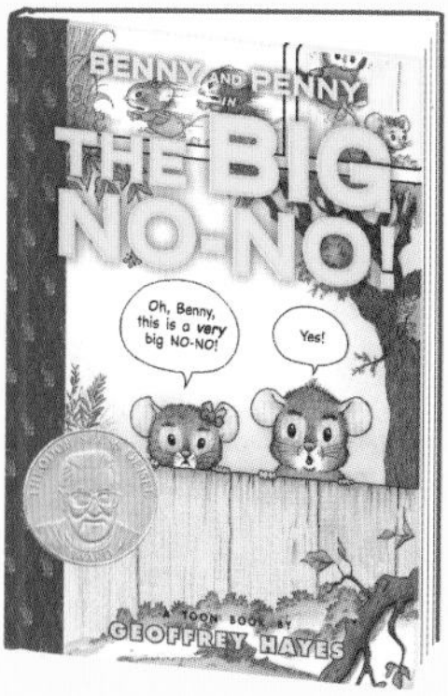

BENNY AND PENNY IN
THE BIG NO-NO!
Oh, Benny, this is a very big NO-NO!
Yes!
A TOON BOOK BY
GEOFFREY HAYES

BENNY AND PENNY
in The Big No-No!
by Geoffrey Hayes

The **TOON INTO READING!**™ program is designed for beginning readers and works wonders with reluctant readers.

Don't miss out on these other Benny and Penny *and other books by Geoffrey Hayes!*

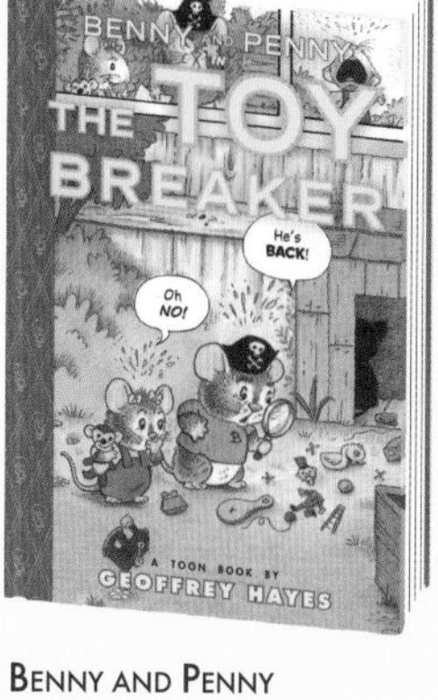

BENNY AND PENNY IN
THE TOY BREAKER
He's BACK!
Oh NO!
A TOON BOOK BY
GEOFFREY HAYES

BENNY AND PENNY
in The Toy Breaker
by Geoffrey Hayes

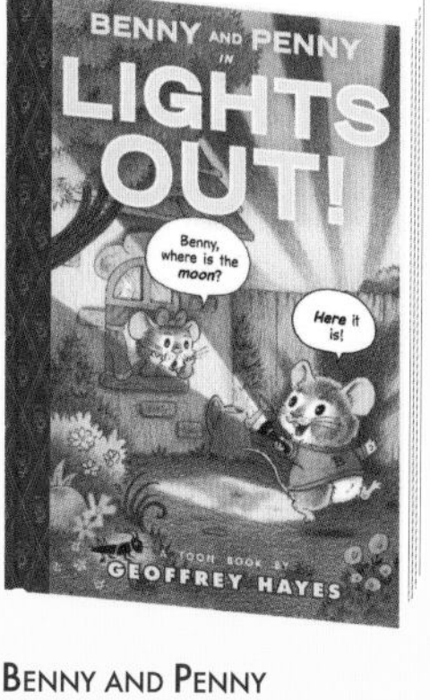

BENNY AND PENNY IN
LIGHTS OUT!
Benny, where is the moon?
Here it is!
A TOON BOOK BY
GEOFFREY HAYES

BENNY AND PENNY
in Lights Out!
by Geoffrey Hayes

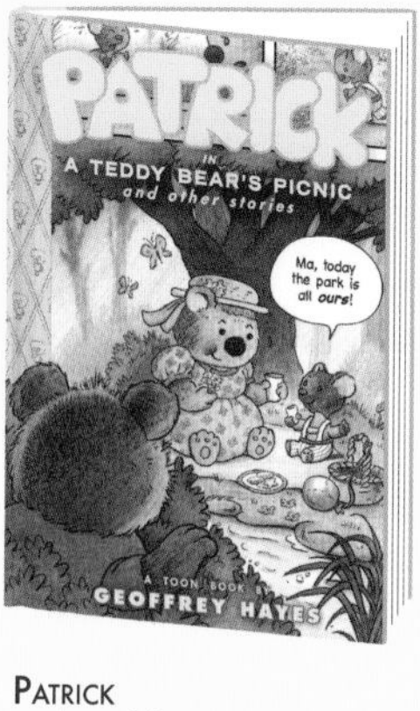

PATRICK
IN A TEDDY BEAR'S PICNIC
and other stories
Ma, today the park is all ours!
A TOON BOOK
GEOFFREY HAYES

PATRICK
in A Teddy Bear's Picnic
by Geoffrey Hayes

2 GUIDE YOUNG READERS

What works?

Keep your fingertip below the character that is speaking.

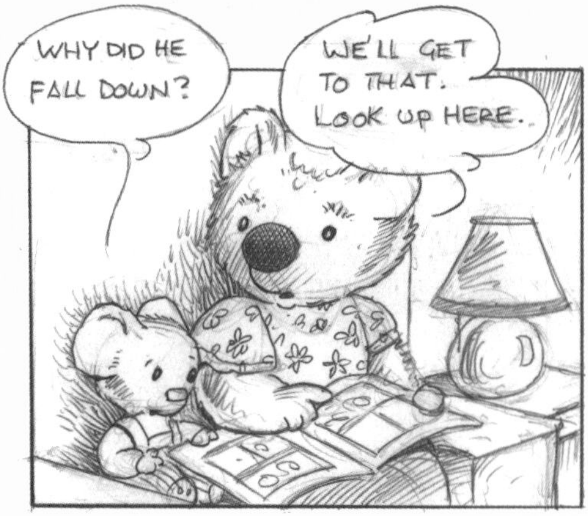
WHY DID HE FALL DOWN?
WE'LL GET TO THAT. LOOK UP HERE.

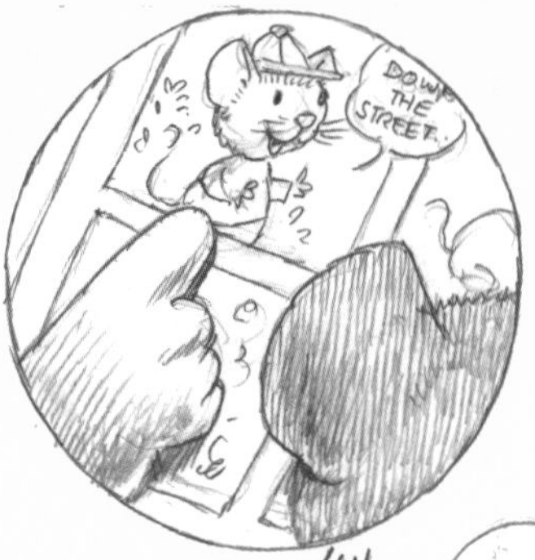
DOWN THE STREET.

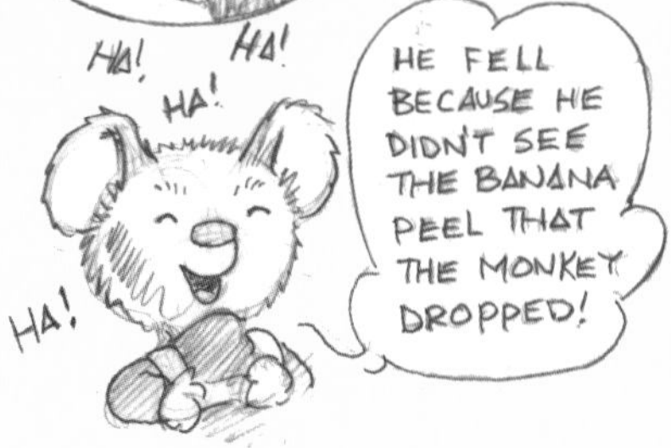
HA! HA! HA! HA!
HE FELL BECAUSE HE DIDN'T SEE THE BANANA PEEL THAT THE MONKEY DROPPED!

3 LET THE PICTURES TELL THE STORY

In a comic, you can often read the story even if you don't know all the words. Encourage young readers to tell you what's happening based on the facial expressions and body language.

4 GET OUT THE CRAYONS

Kids see the hand of the author in a comic and it makes them want to tell their own stories. Encourage them to talk, write and draw!

Get kids talking, and you'll be surprised at how perceptive they are about pictures.

5 LET THEM GUESS

Comics provide a large amount of context for the words, so let young readers make informed guesses, and don't over-correct. In this panel, the artist shows a pirate ship, two pirate hats, and two pirate flags the first time the word "PIRATE" is introduced.

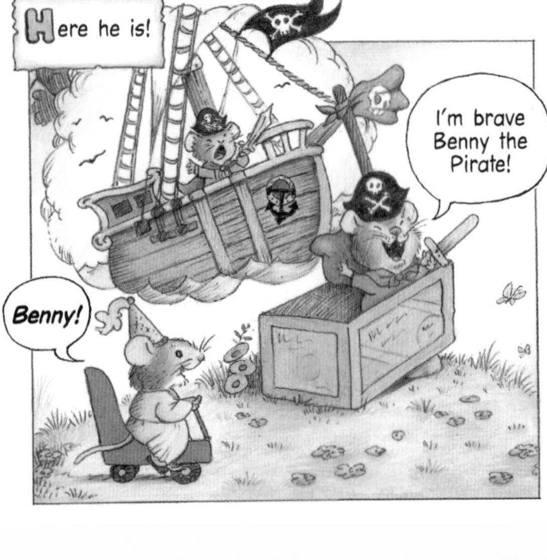
Here he is!
I'm brave Benny the Pirate!
Benny!